The Hearing Trumpet

The Hearing Trumpet

Leonora Carrington

Illustrations by
Pablo Weisz-Carrington

City Lights Books
San Francisco

French edition by Editions Flammarion © 1974
English language version © 1976, 1985 by Leonora Carrington

Library of Congress Cataloging-in-Publication Data

Carrington, Leonora, 1917-
 The hearing trumpet.

 I. Title.
[PR6053.A6965H4 1985] 813 85-19013
ISBN 0-87286-169-4 (pbk.)

CITY LIGHTS BOOKS are edited by Lawrence Ferlinghetti
& Nancy J. Peters and published at the City Lights Bookstore,
261 Columbus Avenue, San Francisco, California 94133.

When Carmella gave me the present of a hearing trumpet she may have foreseen some of the consequences. Carmella is not what I would call malicious, she just happens to have a curious sense of humour. The trumpet was certainly a fine specimen of its kind, without being really modern. It was, however, exceptionally pretty, being encrusted with silver and mother o'pearl motives and grandly curved like a buffalo's horn. The aesthetic presence of this object was not its only quality, the hearing trumpet magnified sound to such a degree that ordinary conversation became quite audible even to my ears.

Here I must say that all my senses are by no means impaired by age. My sight is still excellent although I use spectacles for reading, when I read, which I practically never do. True, rheumatics have bent my skeleton somewhat. This does not prevent me taking a walk in clement weather and sweeping my room once a week, on Thursday, a form of exercise which is both useful and edifying. Here I may add that I consider that I am still a useful member of society and I believe still capable of being pleasant and amusing when the occasion seems fit. The fact that I have no teeth and never could wear dentures does not in any way discomfort me, I don't have to bite anybody and there are all sorts of soft edible foods easy to procure and digestible to the stomach. Mashed vegetables, chocolate and bread dipped in warm water make the base of my simple diet. I never eat meat as I think it is

wrong to deprive animals of their life when they are so difficult to chew anyway.

I am now ninety-two and for some fifteen years I have lived with my son and his family. Our house is situated in a residential district and would be described in England as a semi-detached villa with a small garden. I don't know what they call it here but probably some Spanish equivalent of 'spacious residence with park.' This is untrue, the house is not spacious, it is cramped, there is nothing resembling even faintly a park. There is, however, a fine back yard which I share with my two cats, a hen, the maid and her two children, some flies and a cactus plant called maguey.

My room looks onto this nice back yard which is very convenient as there are no stairs to negotiate—I merely have to open the door in order to enjoy the stars at night or the early morning sun, the only manifestation of sunlight which I can abide. The maid, Rosina, is an Indian woman with a morose character and seems generally opposed to the rest of humanity. I do not believe that she puts me in a human category so our relationship is not disagreeable. The maguey plant, the flies and myself are things which occupy the back yard, we are elements of the landscape and are accepted as such. The cats are another matter. Their individuality puts Rosina into fits of delight or fury according to her temper. She talks to the cats, she never talks to her children at all, although I think she likes them in her own way.

I never could understand this country and now I am beginning to be afraid that I never will get back to the north, never get away from here. I must not give up hope, miracles can happen and very often do happen. People think fifty years is a long time to visit any country because it is often more than half a lifetime. To me fifty years is no more than a space of time stuck somewhere I don't really want to be at all. For the last forty-five years I have been trying to get away. Somehow I never could, there must be a binding spell which keeps me in this country. Sometime I shall find out why I stayed so long here, while I am happily contemplating reindeer and snow, cherry trees, meadows, the song of the thrush.

England is not always the focus of these dreams. I do not, in fact,

particularly want to install myself in England although I will have to visit my mother in London, she is getting old now, although enjoying excellent health. A hundred and ten is not such a great age, from a biblical point of view at least. Margrave, my mother's valet, who sends me post cards of Buckingham Palace, tells me she is still very spry in her wheel chair, although how anyone can be spry in a wheel chair I really don't know. He says she is quite blind but has no beard which must be a reference to a photograph of myself which I sent as a Christmas gift last year.

Indeed I do have a short grey beard which conventional people would find repulsive. Personally I find it rather gallant.

England would be a matter of a few weeks, then I would join my lifelong dream of going to Lapland to be drawn in a vehicle by dogs, woolly dogs.

All this is a digression and I do not wish anyone to think my mind wanders far, it wanders but never further than I want.

So, I live with my Galahad, mostly in the back yard.

Now Galahad has a rather large family and he is by no means rich. He lives on a small wage paid to consular employees, those who are not actually ambassadors. (These, I am told, get a more ample salary from the government.) Galahad is married to the daughter of the manager of a cement factory. Her name is Muriel and both her parents are English. Muriel has five children one of which, the youngest, still lives here with us. This boy, Robert, is twenty-five and has not married yet. Robert is not a pleasant character and even as a child was unkind to cats. He also circulates on a motor cycle and introduced a television set into the house. From that time on my visits to front regions of our residence became increasingly rare. If I ever appear there now it is always rather in the nature of a spectre, if I may say so. This seems to give a certain relief to the rest of the family as my table manners were becoming unconventional. With age one becomes rather less sensitive to the idiosyncrasies of others; for instance at the age of forty I would have hesitated to eat oranges in a crowded tram or bus, today I would not only eat oranges with impunity but I would take an entire meal unblushingly in any public vehicle and wash it

down with a glass of port which I take now and again as a special treat.

Nevertheless I make myself useful and help in the kitchen which is next door to my room. I peel vegetables, feed the hen, and, as I mentioned before, carry out other violent activities like sweeping out my room on Thursdays. I give no trouble at all and keep myself clean with no assistance from anybody.

Every week brings a certain amount of mild enjoyment; every night, in fine weather, the sky, the stars, and of course the moon in her season. On Mondays, in clement weather, I walk two blocks down the road and visit my friend Carmella. She lives in a very small house with her niece who bakes cakes for a Swedish teashop although she is Spanish. Carmella has a very pleasant life and is really very intellectual. She reads books through an elegant lorgnette and hardly ever mumbles to herself as I do. She also knits very clever jumpers but her real pleasure in life is writing letters. Carmella writes letters all over the world to people she has never met and signs them with all sorts of romantic names, never her own. Carmella despises anonymous letters, and of course they would be impractical as who could answer a letter with no name at all signed at the end? These wonderful letters fly off, in a celestial way, by airmail, in Carmella's delicate hand-writing. No one ever replies. This is the really incomprehensible side of humanity, people never have time for anything.

Well one fine Monday morning I went on my usual visit to Carmella who was actually waiting for me on the doorstep. I could see at once that she was in a state of high excitement as she had forgotten to put on her wig. Carmella is bald. She would never go onto the street without her wig on ordinary occasions as she is rather vain, her red wig is a kind of queenly gesture to her long lost hair, which was almost as red as her wig if my memory is correct. This Monday morning Carmella was uncrowned with her usual glory but very excited and mumbling to herself, which is not her ordinary habit. I had brought her an egg which the hen had laid the same morning, I dropped it as she clutched my arm. This was a great pity as the egg was now beyond repair.

"I was waiting for you, Marian, you are twenty minutes late," she said taking no notice of the broken egg. "Some day you will forget to come at all." Her voice was a thin shriek and this was more or less what she said, because of course I did not hear it all. She pulled me inside the house and after several attempts gave me to understand that she had a present for me. "A present, a present, a present." Now Carmella has given me presents several times and they are sometimes knitted and sometimes comestible, but I never saw her so excited. When she unwrapped the hearing trumpet I was at a loss to know whether it could be used for eating or drinking or merely for ornament. After many complicated gestures she finally put it to my ear and what I had always heard as a thin shriek went through my head like the bellow of an angry bull. "Can you hear me Marian?"

Indeed I could, it was terrifying.

"Can you hear me Marian?"

I nodded speechlessly, this frightful noise was worse than Robert's motor cycle.

"This magnificent trumpet is going to change your life."

Finally I said "For goodness sake don't shout you make me nervous."

"A miracle!" said Carmella, still excited, then using a quieter voice, "Your life will be changed."

We both sat down and sucked a violet scented lozenge which Carmella likes because it scents the breath; I am now getting used to the rather nasty taste and beginning to like them through my fondness for Carmella. We thought about all the revolutionary possibilities of the trumpet.

"Not only will you be able to sit and listen to beautiful music and intelligent conversation but you will also have the privilege of being able to spy on what your whole family are saying about you, and that ought to be very amusing." Carmella had finished her lozenge and had lit a small black cigar which she reserves for special occasions. "You must of course be very secretive about the trumpet because they might take it away from you if they don't want you to hear what they are saying."

"Why should they want to hide anything from me?" I asked, thinking about Carmella's incurable passion for drama. "I don't give them any trouble and they almost never see me."

"You never know," said Carmella. "People under seventy and over seven are very unreliable if they are not cats. You can't be too careful. Besides, think of the exhilarating power of listening to others talk when they think you cannot hear."

"They can hardly avoid seeing the trumpet," I said doubtfully. "It must be a buffalo's horn, buffalos are very large animals."

"Of course you must not let them see you using it, you have to hide somewhere and listen." I hadn't thought of that, it certainly promised infinite possibilities.

"Well, Carmella, I think it is very kind of you and this mother o' pearl floral design is very pretty indeed, it looks Jacobean."

"You will also be able to listen to my last letter which I haven't sent yet as I was waiting to read it to you. Ever since I stole the Paris telephone directory from the consulate I have increased my output. You have no ideas of the beautiful names in Paris. This letter is addressed to Monsieur Belvedere Oise Noisis, rue de la Reche Potin, Paris IIe. You could hardly invent anything more sonorous even if you tried. I see him as a rather frail old gentleman, still elegant, with a passion for tropical mushrooms which he grows in an Empire wardrobe. He wears embroidered waistcoats and travels with purple luggage."

"You know Carmella I sometimes think that you might get a reply if you didn't impose your imagination on people you have never seen. Monsieur Belvedere Oise Noisis is undoubtedly a very nice name, but suppose he is fat and collects wicker baskets? Suppose he never travels and has no luggage, suppose he is a young man with a nautical yearning? You must be more realistic I think."

"You are sometimes very negative minded Marian, although I know you have a kind heart, that is no reason that poor Monsieur Belvedere Oise Noisis should do anything so trivial as collecting wicker baskets. He is fragile but intrepid, I intend to send him some mushroom spore to enrich the species which he had sent from the Himalayas." There was no more to be said so Carmella read

the letter. She was pretending to be a famous Peruvian alpinist who had lost an arm trying to save the life of a grisly bear cub trapped on the edge of a precipice. The mother bear had unkindly bitten off her arm. She went on to give all sorts of information about high altitude fungus and offered to send samples. It seemed to me that she took too much for granted.

When I left Carmella's house it was almost lunch-time. I carried my mysterious parcel under my shawl, walking very slowly in order to reserve energy. I was feeling quite excited by this time and had almost forgotten that there was to be tomato soup for lunch. I have always been very fond of tinned tomato soup, we do not have it very often.

My state of slight exhilaration gave me the idea of walking through the front door instead of going around the back way which is my usual procedure. I had a faint idea of stealing one or two chocolates from Muriel which she hides behind the bookcase. Muriel is very mean about sweets and she wouldn't be so fat if she were more generous. I knew she had gone downtown to buy antimacassars to hide grease spots on the chairs. I dislike antimacassars myself and prefer washable wicker chairs which are not so depressing as cloth when dirty. Unfortunately Robert was in the lounge entertaining two of his friends to cocktails. They all stared at me and looked away quickly when I began explaining that I had been for my usual Monday walk. My diction is not quite as good as it used to be because of having no teeth. My monologue had not gone on for long when Robert took me roughly by the arm and ejected me into the passage leading to the kitchen. It was obvious that he was angry. As Carmella says, one can never trust people under seventy and over seven.

As usual I ate lunch in the kitchen and went to my room to comb Marmeen and Tchatcha, the cats. I comb the cats every day in order to keep their long fur smart and glossy and to reserve the hair I get off the combs for Carmella, who has promised to knit it into a jumper when there is enough. I have now filled two small jam jars with the nice soft hair. It seems a pleasant and economical way of having warm clothing for the winter. Carmella thinks that a

7

sleeveless cardigan is a practical garment for cold weather. I have been four years now filling the two jars so it may take some time to get enough wool to make a complete garment. It might be possible to weave a little lama wool with it, although Carmella says that would be cheating. Rosina's cousin once brought me the present of a simple Indian spinning wheel. I have been trying it out on cotton waste and spinning nice useful ropes. By the time I have enough cat's wool to spin I shall have learnt enough to spin fine yarn. This is an enterprising occupation and I must say I would be fairly happy if I did not feel so much nostalgia for the north. They say you can see the pole star from here and that it never moves. I have never been able to find it. Carmella has a planisphere but we cannot discover how to use it, and there are so few people one can consult on such matters.

When I had hidden the hearing trumpet carefully I set about my afternoon's work.

The red hen looked as if she was laying another egg on my bed and Marmeen was objecting to having his tail combed out, all as usual. The sudden apparition of Galahad in the room almost knocked me off my chair. The last time my son visited me was when the tank burst and he came in with the plumber. He stood mouthing in the door. I suppose he was saying something.

Then he put a bottle of port wine on my chest of drawers, mouthed some more and left. This astonishing behaviour from Galahad left me pensive till evening. There was no reason I could think of to explain his visit. It was not my birthday, and he never gave me a birthday present; judging from the weather it was not Christmas. Why should he make such extravagant changes in his habits?

At that time I do not think I attributed any ominous interpretation to the event, I was merely curious and surprised. Of course if I had Carmella's gift of perceptive psychology I might, even then, have been a little preoccupied. In any case even if I had foreseen the events that followed there was nothing I could have done except wait.

A great deal of my life has been spent in waiting, most of it quite

fruitless. Recently I do not go in for much coherent thought, however on that occasion I actually made a plan of action. I wanted to find out the motives for Galahad's unwonted kindness. Not that he lacks ordinary human sentiment, simply that he considers kindness to inanimate creatures a waste of time. He may be right, but on the other hand the maguey cactus seems alive to me, so I feel I can also make claims on existence.

When the evening drew on and dinner time was past I waited for Rosina to retire and then, unwrapping my hearing trumpet carefully, I left my room and went and hid in the dark passage between the lounge and the kitchen. The door here was always open so I had no trouble taking in a nice picture of family life. Galahad was sitting opposite Muriel near the fireplace which had an electric log. This was out, as the weather was not too chilly. Robert was sitting on the narrow sofa tearing the morning paper into strips. The new antimacassars were hanging dutifully on the chairs and sofa. They were dark beige with fringes, practical I suppose, and easy to wash. The three members of my family were engaged in some sort of discussion.

"Even if it never happens again the result is intolerable," said Robert, so loudly my trumpet vibrated. "I shall never dare invite any of my friends here again."

"I thought everything was already decided," said Galahad. "You don't have to go on being so excited when we have all agreed that she would be much better off in a home."

"You always decide everything twenty years too late," said Muriel. "Your mother has been a constant anxiety to us for the past twenty years and you have been stubborn and inert enough to keep her here on our hands just to satisfy your own sentimentality."

"Muriel, you are being unfair," said Galahad weakly. "You know we never had the means of keeping her in an institution before Charles died."

"The government provides institutions for the aged and infirm," snapped Muriel. "She ought to have been put away long ago."

"We are not in England," said Galahad. "Institutions here are not fit for human beings."

"Grandmother," said Robert, "can hardly be classified as a human being. She's a drooling sack of decomposing flesh."

"Robert," said Galahad without conviction, "really, Robert."

"Well I've had enough," said Robert. "Inviting people here for a normal chat and a drink and in walks the monster of Glamis, gibbering at us in broad daylight until I have to throw her out. Gently of course."

"Remember Galahad," added Muriel, "these old people do not have feelings like you or I. She would be much happier in an institution where there's proper help to take care of her. They are very well organized today. This place I told you about out in Santa Brigida is run by the Well of Light Brotherhood and they are financed by a prominent American Cereal company (Bouncing Breakfast Cereals Co.). It is all very efficiently organized and reasonably inexpensive."

"Yes you told me," said Galahad who seemed bored by the discussion. "I agree it seems the sort of place to send her, she will be quite well cared for there I expect."

"So when do we pack her off?" said Robert. "I could turn that room into a work shop for the motor bike."

"There's no desperate hurry," said Galahad. "She will have to be told."

"Told?" said Muriel in surprise. "She doesn't have any idea where she is, I don't think she will even notice the change."

"She might," said Galahad. "You never can tell how much she understands about anything."

"Your mother," replied Muriel, "is senile. The sooner you accept that the better."

For a moment I took the trumpet away from my ear, partially because my arm ached. Senile? yes I dare say they were right, but what does senile mean?

I applied the trumpet again to the other ear, "She ought to be dead," Robert said. "At that age people are better off dead."

Back in bed wearing my woolen night shirt I found myself

trembling with an ague that seemed to belong to someone else. The dreadful recurrent thought was first: "The cats, what will become of the cats? then Carmella, what about Carmella on a Monday morning, and the red hen? and why do they suppose they know that one is better off dead? how can they possibly know that? and o Dear Venus (I always pray to Venus, she is such a brilliant and recognisable star) what is the 'Well of Light Brotherhood?' that sounds more terrifying than death itself, a Brotherhood with the grim knowledge of what is better for other people and the iron determination to better them whether they like it or not. O Venus, what have I done to deserve that? and what about the cats, what will become of Marmeen and Tchatcha? I shall never spin their wool into a cardigan to warm my bones, I will never wear cat's wool, I shall probably have to wear a uniform, no red hen to lay a daily egg on my bed."

Tormented by all these horrible visions and thoughts I dropped into something nearer to catalepsy than sleep.

Naturally I visited Carmella the next day to tell her the dreadful news. I took my hearing trumpet, as I hoped for some advice.

"There are times," said Carmella, "when I am clairvoyante. When I saw that trumpet in the flea market I said to myself 'that is just the right thing for Marian.' I had to buy it at once, I had a premonition. This is terrible news, I must try and think of some plan."

"What do you feel about the Well of Light Brotherhood?" I asked. "It frightens me."

"The Well of Light Brotherhood," said Carmella, "is obviously something extremely sinister. Not I suppose a company for grinding old ladies into breakfast cereal, but something morally sinister. It all sounds terrible. I must think of something to save you from the jaws of the Well of Light." This seemed to amuse her for no reason at all and she chuckled although I could see she was quite upset.

"They will not allow me to take the cats you think?"

"No cats," said Carmella. "Institutions, in fact, are not allowed to like anything. They don't have time."

"What shall I do?" I said. "It seems a pity to commit suicide when I have lived for ninety-two years and really haven't understood anything."

"You might escape to Lapland," said Carmella. "We could knit a tent here so you wouldn't have to buy one when you arrived."

"I have no money, I could never get to Lapland without money."

"Money is a great nuisance," said Carmella. "If I had any I would give you some and we would take a holiday on the Riviera on the way to Lapland. We could even gamble a little."

Even Carmella had no practical advice.

Houses are really bodies. We connect ourselves with walls, roofs, and objects just as we hang on to our livers, skeletons, flesh and blood stream. I am no beauty, no mirror is necessary to assure me of this absolute fact. Nevertheless I have a death grip on this haggard frame as if it were the limpid body of Venus herself. This is true of the back yard and the small room I occupied at that time, my body, the cats, the red hen all my body all part of my own sluggish blood stream. A separation from these well-known and loved, yes loved, things were "Death and Death indeed" according to the old rhyme of the Man of Double Deed. There was no remedy for the needle in my heart with its long thread of old blood. Then what about Lapland and the furry dog team? That would also be a fine violation of those cherished habits, yes indeed, but how different from an institution for decrepit old women.

"In case they lock you up in a tenth storey room," said Carmella lighting a cigar, "you could take a lot of those ropes you weave, and escape. I could be waiting down below with a machine gun and an automobile, a hired automobile you know, I don't suppose it would be too expensive for an hour or two."

"Where would you get the machine gun?" I asked, intrigued at the idea of Carmella armed with such a deadly artefact. "And how do they work? We never succeeded in operating that planisphere. I must suppose that a machine gun would be more complicated."

"Machine guns," said Carmella, "are simplicity itself. You load them with a lot of bullets and press a trigger. There is no

intellectual manipulation necessary and you don't have to actually hit anything. The noise impresses people, they think you are dangerous if you have a machine gun."

"You might well be dangerous," I replied alarmed. "Supposing you hit me by mistake?"

"I would only press the trigger in case of absolute necessity. They might turn a pack of police dogs on us in which case I should be obliged to shoot. A whole pack of dogs is quite a large target, forty dogs at a distance of three yards would not be difficult to hit. I could always tell you apart from an angry police hound."

I could not feel quite happy about Carmella's argument, "Supposing there was only one police dog chasing me around and around in circles. You might easily hit me instead of the hound."

"You," said Carmella stabbing the air with her cigar, "would be swarming down ten stories on your rope. The hounds would be attacking me, not you."

"Well," I said still not quite convinced, "after we had left the exercise yard (it would be an exercise yard I suppose, surrounded by high walls), littered with dead police dogs, what would we do then and where would we go?"

"We would join the gang at an expensive seaside resort and go on tapping telephone wires for horse race winners before the bookies pay out."

Carmella was off on a tangent. I made an attempt to bring her back to the point of our discussion.

"I thought you said animals were not allowed in institutions. Forty police dogs are surely animals?"

"Police dogs are not properly speaking animals. Police dogs are perverted animals with no animal mentality. Policemen are not human beings so how can police dogs be animals?"

This was impossible to answer. Carmella ought to have been a lawyer, she was so good at complicated debate.

"You might just as well say that collie dogs are perverted sheep," I said eventually. "If they keep so many dogs in an institution I don't see what difference a cat or two would make."

"Think of the cats living in constant anguish amongst forty ferocious police hounds."

Carmella stared in front of her with an agonized expression, "Their nervous systems would not survive a situation like that." She was right, of course, as usual.

Still feeling crushed with despair I hobbled back home. How I would miss Carmella and her stimulating advice, the black cigars, the violet lozenges. They would probably make me suck vitamins in an institution. Vitamins and police hounds, grey walls, machine guns. I could not think coherently, the horror of the situation floated in tangled masses in my head, making it ache as if it was stuffed with thorny seaweed.

Force of habit rather than my own capacity carried me home and sat me down in the back yard. Strangely enough I was in England and it was Sunday afternoon. I was sitting with a book on a stone seat under a lilac bush. Close by a clump of rosemary saturated the air with perfume. They were playing tennis nearby, the clump clump of the rackets and balls was quite audible. This was the sunken Dutch garden, why Dutch I wonder? The roses? the geometrical flower beds? or perhaps because it is sunken? The church bells ringing, that is the Protestant church, have we had tea yet? (cucumber sandwiches, seed cake and rock buns) Yes, tea must be over.

My long dark hair is soft like cat's fur, I am beautiful. This is quite a shock because I have just realised that I am beautiful and there is something that I must do about it, but what? Beauty is a responsibility like anything else, beautiful women have special lives like prime ministers but that is not what I really want, there must be something else . . . The book. Now I can see it, the Tales of Hans Christian Andersen, the Snow Queen.

The Snow Queen, Lapland. Little Kay doing multiplication problems in the icy castle.

Now I can see that I also was given a mathematical problem which I cannot solve although I seem to have been trying for many many years. I am not really here in England in this scented garden although it does not disappear as it nearly always does, I am inventing all this and it is about to disappear, but it does not. Feeling so strong and happy is very dangerous, something horrible is about to happen and I must find the solution quickly.

All the things I love are going to disintegrate and there is nothing I can do about it unless I can solve the Snow Queen's problem. She is the Sphinx of the North with crackling white fur and diamonds on the ten claws of every foot, her smile is frozen and her tears rattle like hail on the strange diagrams drawn at her feet. Somewhere, sometime, I must have betrayed the Snow Queen, for surely by now I should know?

The young man wearing white flannels has come to ask me something, am I going to play tennis? well, I am not really very good you know, that is why I prefer to read a book. No, not an intellectual book, just fairy tales. Fairy tales at your age?

Why not? What is age anyway? Something you don't understand, My Love.

The woods are full of wild anemones now, shall we go? no Darling, I didn't say wild enemas, I said wild anemones, flowers, hundreds and thousands of wild flowers all over the ground under the trees all the way up to the gazebo. They have no smell but they have a presence just like a perfume and quite as obsessive, I shall remember them all my life.

Are you going somewhere Darling?

Yes, going to the woods.

Then why do you say you will remember them all your life?

Because you are part of their memory and you are going to disappear, the anemones are going to blossom eternally, we are not.

Darling stop being philosophical it doesn't suit you, it makes your nose red.

Since I discovered that I am really beautiful I don't care about having a red nose it is such a beautiful shape.

You are hatefully vain.

No Darling, not really because I have a frightful foreboding that it will disappear before I know what to do with it. I am so horribly afraid I don't have time to enjoy being vain.

You are a depressive maniac and I would be bored stiff if you were not so pretty.

Nobody could ever be bored with me I have too much soul.

Far too much, but lots of body too, thank Heavens. The green and gold light in the woods, look at the great ferns. They say witches make magic with fern seeds, they are hermaphrodites.

The witches?

No the ferns. Somebody brought that colossal bluish fir tree from Canada, it cost millions and millions, how silly to bring a tree from America. Don't you hate America?

No, why should I hate America, I've never been there, they are frightfully civilised.

Well I hate America because I know that once you get in you can never get out and you go on crying all your life for the anemones you will never see again.

Perhaps America is covered from head to foot with wild flowers, mostly anemones of course.

I know it is not.

How can you possibly know that?

Not the part of America I am thinking about. They have other sorts of plants, and dust. Dust, dust. Probably a few palm trees and cowboys galloping hither and thither on cows.

They ride horses.

Well horses. Does it matter when you are so sick to get home again that you wouldn't notice if they were riding cockroaches?

Well you don't have to go to America, so cheer up.

Don't I? Who knows, something tells me that I am going to see a lot of America and I am going to be very sad there unless a miracle happens.

Miracles, witches, fairy tales, grow up Darling!

You may not believe in magic but something very strange is happening at this very moment. Your head has dissolved into thin air and I can see the rhododendrons through your stomach. It's not that you are dead or anything dramatic like that, it is simply that you are fading away and I can't even remember your name. I remember your white flannels better than I can remember you. I remember all the things I felt about the white flannels but whoever made them walk about has totally disappeared.

So you remember me as a pink linen dress with no sleeves and

17

my face is confused with dozens of other faces, I have no name either. So why so much fuss about individuality?

I thought I heard the Snow Queen laugh, she seldom laughs.

There I was nodding away in my terrible old carcass and Galahad was trying to tell me something. He was shouting at the top of his voice: "No, I am not inviting you to play tennis, I am trying to tell you something very agreeable and important."

Agreeable? Important?

"You are going away on a nice holiday, mother. You are going to enjoy it very much."

"My dear Galahad, don't tell me such silly lies. You are sending me away to a home for senile females because you all think I am a repulsive old bag and I dare say you are right from your own point of view."

He stood mouthing at me, looking as if I had picked a live goat out of my bonnet.

"We expect you to be reasonable about all this," he yelled eventually, "You will be very comfortable and have a lot of company."

"My dear Galahad, I wonder what you consider being unreasonable? Do you mean that I might tear the house down brick by brick and stamp on it? Throw the television set off the roof? Ride off naked on Robert's revolting motor cycle? No, Galahad. I do not have the strength for any of these reactions. I have absolutely no choice except being what you call reasonable, you need not worry."

"You will find that you will be very happy mother, you will have all sorts of interesting pastimes and a trained staff to see that you are never lonely."

"I am never lonely, Galahad. Or rather I never suffer from loneliness. I suffer much from the idea that my loneliness might be taken away from me by a lot of mercilessly well meaning people. Of course I never hope that you will understand me, so all I ask is that you do not imagine that you are persuading me into something when you are actually forcing me against my will."

"Really mother, it will be for your own good, I know you will appreciate this later on."

"I doubt it very much. However, nothing I can say will change your opinion, so when do I have to go?"

"Well we thought we might drive you out on Tuesday, just to have a look at things. If you are not pleased with the place you can come right home again."

"Today is Sunday."

"Yes today is Sunday. I am glad to see you perking up mother, you'll see what a fine time you are going to have making lots of friends and taking healthy exercise out in Santa Brigida. It is almost the country you know."

"What do you mean 'healthy exercise?' " I asked, prey to an awful premonition that they might have a hockey team; one never knows with modern therapy. "I get plenty of exercise here."

"Organized sports of some sort," replied Galahad, confirming my fears. "You are going to feel like a two-year old after a month or two."

I didn't seem able to get my breath properly, I held my peace in order to reserve energy, I had too many things to find out before falling stark into a grave. Besides argument with Galahad was obviously unfruitful. He went on talking for some time but I no longer heard what he said as he wasn't shouting any more.

Some fifty or sixty years ago I bought a practical tin trunk in the Jewish quarter in New York. This trunk has resisted time in all sorts of different services. Recently I had used it as a tea-table when Carmella came to visit me. I had only expected to pack it again when I would leave for Lapland. One can never be sure of the future. I had not opened the trunk for about seven years, that must have been the time Carmella gave me a bottle of sleeping potion that she made herself and that I never dared to taste. The bottle was still lying at the bottom of the trunk and had turned into a crystalline sediment which looked extraordinarily venemous, having a brownish tint with a grey fungoid growth around the top. I decided to keep it just the same, one never can know what might be useful, I never throw anything away. The trunk inside was made of solid wood and papered with a tasteful design which was slightly stained in places.

The first object I packed next to the sleeping potion was of

course the fatal hearing trumpet. This made me think of the Angel Gabriel although I believe he is supposed to blow his and not listen through it, that is, according to the bible, on the last day when humanity rises to ultimate catastrophe. Strange how the bible always seems to end up in misery and cataclysm. I often wondered how their angry and vicious God became so popular. Humanity is very strange and I don't pretend to understand anything, however why worship something that only sends you plagues and massacres? and why was Eve blamed for everything?

Then I had to open the chest of drawers and sort things out, and all the cardboard boxes with different labels, marmalade, glass, tinned beans, tomato ketchup. They did not, of course, contain what the labels said, but different odds and ends which agglomerate with time.

One has to be very careful what one takes when one goes away forever, something seemingly useless might become essential under specific circumstances. I decided to pack as if I were going to Lapland. There was a screw driver, hammer, nails, birdseed, a lot of ropes that I had woven myself, some strips of leather, part of an alarm clock, needles and thread, a bag of sugar, matches, coloured beads, sea shells and so on. Finally I put in a few clothes to prevent things rattling about inside the trunk.

Knowing Muriel to be an officious Nosey Parker and wanting to prevent any possible revision of my belongings, I filled the empty cardboard boxes with stones from the back yard and tied them up again with string, so that she would think I had left all my miscellaneous collection behind. Muriel would call it all "rubbish" and throw it away.

Of course I knew I was not going to bribe the Eskimos, but I put everything in as if I were. Institutions like the far north are also cut off from civilization and you never know what people might want. I was not educated in a convent school for nothing.

Time, as we all know, passes. Whether it returns in quite the same way is doubtful. A friend of mine who I did not mention up till now because of his absence told me that a pink and a blue universe cross each other in particles like two swarms of bees and

when a pair of different coloured bees hit each other miracles happen. All this has something to do with time although I doubt if I could explain it coherently.

This particular friend, Mr. Marlborough, has been living in Venice with his sister so I haven't seen him for some time. Mr. Marlborough is a great poet and has achieved fame in recent years. At times I had thought of writing poetry myself but getting words to rhyme with each other is difficult, like trying to drive a herd of turkeys and kangaroos down a crowded thoroughfare and keep them neatly together without looking in shop windows. There are so many words, and they all mean something. Marlborough tells me his sister has been a cripple from birth although he says it so mysteriously I sometimes wonder what is really the matter with her.

If I remember correctly writers usually find some excuse for their books, although why one should excuse oneself for having such a quiet and peaceful occupation I really don't know. Military people never seem to apologize for killing each other yet novelists feel ashamed for writing some nice inert paper book that is not certain to be read by anybody. Values are very strange, they change so quickly I can't keep track of them.

I say all this because I think I might write some poetry after all. I think a ballad would be rather in my style, with short simple verses, such as:

> 'Not a thing upon the floor,
> Although I looked from door to door.
> Abandoned by my kith and kin
> I'll leave them not a safety pin.'

Not anything pretentious with long words. This is merely an example, as I would actually favour something more romantic.

With all these thoughts running through my head like sand through a sieve I continued my packing. It was quite a long job but I had no desire to sleep, I was too preoccupied.

Sleeping and waking are not quite as distinctive as they used to be, I often mix them up. My memory is full of all sorts of stuff

which is not, perhaps, in chronological order, but there is a lot of it. So I pride myself on having an excellent faculty of miscellaneous recall.

> The cats were singing hymns to the moon,
> On the seashore just a silver spoon,

This rhyming image never was finished, I must have dropped off to sleep after all.

Santa Brigida is a suburb on the southern extremity of this city. Actually it is an ancient Indian-Spanish village linked by petrol stations and factories to the metropolis. The houses are sometimes of adobe and sometimes of massive stone, the streets are roughly paved and narrow, bordered with trees and high walls hiding colonial mansions and parks. The place would have a certain charm if it did not smell so strongly on wet days of the paper factory, Gomez and Company. A drop of rain and the whole place is invaded by a frightful stink.

The last house on Calle Albahacca was the Institution. It was quite unlike anything that either Carmella or I had imagined. There were walls, naturally, but otherwise everything was different. Outside nothing much could be seen except great old walls over which dripped plumbago and ivy. The front door was a massive lump of wood studded with iron lumps that might once have been heads. They were rubbed almost smooth. I could just see a tower jutting about a storey over the wall. All this looked more like a medieval castle than the hospital or prison I had expected.

The lady who let us in was so surprisingly different from the immaculate keeper I had expected that I could not stop looking at her. She was somewhat younger than myself, about ten years say; she wore a pair of flannel pyjama trousers, a gentleman's dinner jacket and a grey, turtlenecked sweater. She had rather a lot of hair which straggled out from under a yachting cap which bore the words H.M.S. Thumbelina, and a crown. She seemed very excited and never stopped talking. Galahad and Muriel tried to make a

remark now and then and she did not let them get a word in edgeways.

First impressions are never very clear, I can only say there seemed to be several court yards, cloisters, stagnant fountains, trees, shrubs, lawns. The main building was in fact a castle, surrounded by various pavilions with incongruous shapes. Pixielike dwellings shaped like toadstools, swiss chalets, railway carriages, one or two ordinary bungalows, something shaped like a boot, another like what I took to be an outsize Egyptian mummy. It was all so very strange that I for once doubted the accuracy of my observation. Our guide went on talking excitedly and seemed to be explaining something to me, she ignored Muriel and Galahad. I could see astonishment written all over their faces, but the fact that they had taken the trouble to bring my trunk prevented them from changing their minds.

After walking for a long time we got to a tower which was standing alone in a vegetable garden. This was not the tower of the main building. It was a new tower and not more than three stories tall and whitewashed. It had a certain resemblance to a lighthouse, hardly what one would expect in a garden. Our guide opened the door and, after talking for a quarter of an hour, let us in. This extraordinary place was evidently where I was supposed to live. The only real furniture was a wicker chair and a small table. All the rest was painted. What I mean is that the walls were painted with the furniture that wasn't there. It was so clever that I was almost taken in at first. I tried to open the painted wardrobe, a book-case with books and their titles. An open window with a curtain fluttering in the breeze, or rather it would have fluttered if it were a real curtain. A painted door and a shelf with all sorts of ornaments. All this one-dimensional furniture had a strangely depressing effect, like banging one's nose against a glass door.

It was not long before Galahad and Muriel left, but our companion stayed on, talking like mad. I wondered if she knew that I could not hear a word she said. But it would have been impossible to communicate anything through the torrent of words, even if my annunciation had been loud and strong. Finally I

left her alone still talking and climbed up the stairs to examine the rest of the tower. There was a room with a real window, a bed and a closet. The walls were undecorated. In the corner was a ladder leading to a trap door which I decided to leave for another occasion, as I felt rather weak from so much exertion.

I was able to make twenty-five trips up and down stairs and unpack my entire trunk and she was still talking. I decided I might risk using my hearing trumpet. The bathroom was on the ground floor and was a good spot for testing acoustics.

"Not that it would make a great deal of difference because he was not allowed here in any case because of the ducks. He sent me a fine long letter, though, and you should have read how he chased a jackal for ten kilometres.

"It is almost teatime now and Dr. Gambit expects us to be assembled before the bell rings. Dr. Gambit is a highly unreasonable person concerning time so we had better hurry. Personally I think that time is unimportant and when I think of the autumn leaves and the snow, the spring and the summer, the birds and the bees I realise that time is unimportant, yet people attach so much importance to clocks. Now I believe in inspiration, an inspired conversation between two people with some mysterious affinity can bring more joy into life than even the most expensive kind of clock. Unfortunately there are very few inspired people and one has to fall back on one's own store of vital fire, this is most exhausting especially, as you know, I have to work day and night even if all my bones ache and my head is swimming and I am fainting with fatigue and nobody understands my mortal fight to keep on my feet and not to lose my inspired joy of life even if I do have palpitations of the heart and they drive me like a poor beast of burden I often feel like Joan of Arc so dreadfully misunderstood and all those terrible cardinals and bishops prodding her poor agonized mind with so many unnecessary questions. I can't help feeling some deep affinity with Joan of Arc and I often feel I am being burned at the stake just because I am different from everybody else because I have always refused to give up that wonderful strange power I have inside me and it becomes

manifested when I am in harmonious communication with some other inspired being like myself."

I made several futile attempts to tell her that I heartily agreed with her philosophy of life. I also wanted to ask if I might bring my hearing trumpet in to tea without exciting too much commentary but it was impossible, she went right on talking although I stood in front of her opening and shutting my mouth hopefully. I was also beginning to worry about the Dr. Gambit who disliked people being late for tea but my companion showed no signs of moving and she stood blocking the only exit. We might get no tea at all if we did not go immediately. This would be very unpleasant. Supposing they only gave high tea and no supper, I would have to go hungry till breakfast.

"If only people in this world realized the importance of understanding each other. Now take me, nobody understands me here, they don't even make an effort to take a small share of the terrible burden of work which is crushing me down like Joan of Arc. Yet my source of inspiration is still untouched because of the fighting power inside me. Bubbles of pure creative ideas pouring out of me, I give, give, give, yet other people do not share this faculty of understanding. More and more work is poured upon me, when I get up in the mornings J am overcome with a terrible nausea because I am overworked, simple overwork is enough to bleed you dry. I am so foolishly generous that other people profit from me all the time and all the endless tasks of the day (and night) are heaped on my shoulders."

This was most alarming, what sort of terrible toil had deranged the poor woman? Would I also have to work day and night till I couldn't stop talking? Perhaps they made her shovel coal for a huge furnace, probably they kept a private crematorium, old people do keep dying off. Maybe they had a chain gang too and we would have to chop stones and sing sea shanties (this would explain why she wore the yachting cap). All those eccentric huts outside began to take on a sinister meaning. Nursery rhyme bungalows to trick the old ladies' families into thinking we led a childish and peaceful life and behind the scenes a huge crematorium and a chain gang.

I began to feel ill and not to mind if we missed tea after all. My arm was paralyzed with holding the hearing trumpet but some kind of unhappy fascination prevented me from taking it away and sinking back into what now seemed like blissful silence. Somewhere in the distance a bell rang and, still talking, my companion took me by the arm and we set out towards the main building. I held the trumpet to my ear as if hypnotized. Her talk was like the wheel of fortune that has certain variations but always gets back to the same point. Her enthusiasm never flagged, nor did her pleasant wrinkled face change its expression of intense sincerity.

Later on I learned that my companion's name was Anna Wertz. She did not tell me this herself as she would never have had time to communicate anything so practical and banal.

The dining hall was a long panelled room with French windows leading out into the garden. Green velvet curtains somewhat the worse for wear separated us from a big lounge in which everything was covered with chintz. We arrived just in time to take our places as everybody sat down. I was placed between Anna Wertz and another lady. We were sitting in the row with our backs to the French windows and this gave me a feeling of claustrophobia.

For a day or two the nine personalities of my new companions were somewhat confused. They were all quite different of course, but it takes time to tell people apart. After a first brief examination I did not dare look too closely at Dr. Gambit, as I was afraid to appear rude. He sat at the head of the table, which was natural I suppose, he being the only gentleman present.

The first impression he gave was of being bald, almost starkly bald, very plump and nervous. It was difficult to see his eyes as he wore very thick spectacles. When I did eventually manage to peep behind these thick lenses I saw he had mild green eyes with dark lashes, rather incongruous in such a face; they looked like the eyes of a child. They were eyes that looked at nothing. I suppose he was so short-sighted that there was nothing much he could see anyhow, poor man.

We were no sooner sitting in front of our ration of strawberry

jam and two slices of bread than Anna Wertz immediately launched into something that may have been a speech.

"Silence, Anna Wertz, hold your peace," said Dr. Gambit so suddenly and in such a penetrating nasal voice that I dropped my spoon. Even without the trumpet I could hear him perfectly.

"Today for the benefit of a new member of Our Little Society I shall outline the basic principles of Lightsome Hall. Most of you have been here for some time and are thoroughly acquainted with our Purpose. We seek to follow the inner Meaning of Christianity and comprehend the Original Teaching of the Master. You have heard me repeating these phrases many, many times, yet do we really grasp the meaning of such Work? Work it is and Work it shall remain. Before we begin to get even a faint glimmer of Truth we must strive for many years and lose hope time and time again before the first recompense is awarded us."

I noticed that he had a slightly foreign accent which was difficult to place. Nevertheless his nasal voice was as audible as any siren. He seemed to inspire everybody with great respect, they all chewed their food and looked at their plates with serious faces.

While he spoke I was able to examine a large oil painting on the wall facing me. The painting represented a nun with a very strange and malicious face.

"These apparently simple, though infinitely difficult, principles are the core of Our Teaching," went on Dr. Gambit. "There are two little words which will ever supply the Key to the understanding of Inner Christianity. Self Remembering, my friends, are the words which we must strive to keep present through all our daily activities."

The face of the Nun in the oil painting was so curiously lighted that she seemed to be winking, although that was hardly possible. She must have had one blind eye and the painter had rendered her infirmity realistically. However the idea that she was winking persisted, she was winking at me with a most disconcerting mixture of mockery and malevolence.

"Self Remembering must not, however," continued the Doctor, "make us into dreary fanatics. We can remember Ourselves and be excellent and merry companions at the same

time." The thought of Dr. Gambit being merry was rather frightening so I stole a look at Anna Wertz to dissipate the image. She was staring at her plate, looking absolutely furious.

One or two ladies asked Dr. Gambit questions and I timidly applied my hearing trumpet so they could see I was taking an intelligent interest. The first lady who spoke was wearing a rather smart striped blouse and waistcoat and had her hair cropped like a man. Later I found out she was a French Marquise called Claude la Checherelle. This impressed me deeply as I had only met a few aristocrats during my life.

"Should we try to Self Remember while playing snakes and ladders?" she asked.

"We Self Remember at all hours and at all occupations or recreations," replied the doctor. I noticed that his spectacles gave a keen glance at my trumpet.

A small woman with a worried expression and sparse fluffy hair was the next one to speak. I could see she was fighting down her embarrassment. "You know Doctor, I do indeed make efforts but I keep on forgetting to Remember Myself, it is most humiliating."

"The very fact that you observe this fault in your own character is already an improvement," said Dr. Gambit, "We Remember Ourselves in order to try and create objective observation of Personality."

"Well I will go on trying most sincerely to improve although I do realize I have a dreadfully weak nature." She was, however, looking very pleased. I wondered if she had made her own blouse, which was pink with a blue bow at the neck. I always admired people who know how to sew. Carmella was an admirable needlewoman. But it was better not to think about Carmella yet.

They were getting up from the table and I just had time to cram the last morsel of bread in my mouth before I was addressed by the French Marquise. "Claude la Checherelle," she said, extending her hand in a frank and friendly manner. If I had known then that she was a Marquise I would have been embarrassed to have my mouth full, however I didn't know, so I swallowed the bread without choking and said "Good Afternoon" politely.

"Let me tell you," she said, taking me firmly by the arm, "how

we defeated the German army in Africa back in forty-one. It was many years ago but the memory is still vivid. . . ."

So that was a typical teatime assembly at Hall. There are few human activities which are typical for any length of time, however.

Three days passed before I had my first private interview with Dr. Gambit. During that time I began to sort out the identity of my other companions and even to get to know them a little. Altogether there were ten of us aged over seventy and under a hundred. The oldest inhabitant was ninety-eight. Her name was Veronica Adams. She had been an artist in her time and still continued to paint water colours although she was totally blind. The fact that she couldn't see what she was doing did not prevent her making a large production of work on the coarse toilet paper provided for our use. She could measure a yard a day and in this manner did not always paint over what she had done the day before.

After Veronica in order of age came Christabel Burns, Georgina Sykes, Natacha Gonzalez, Claude la Checherelle, (The Marquise I already mentioned) Maude Wilkins, Vera Van Tocht, Anna Wertz.

Our daily activity was supervised by Mrs. Gambit, who was lying down most of the time with a sick headache, so we got along on our own. Whenever she appeared, however, the atmosphere became noticeably tense. We were all afraid of her in spite of her constant smile.

Apart from Dr. and Mrs. Gambit and three servants nobody, apparently, lived in the main building. We all occupied our individual huts, or bungalows as they were called. It was several weeks before I learned who lived in the tower of the castle and by that time I knew everybody and the huts allotted to them; everybody, except the person who lived in the tower.

Veronica Adams lived in the boot-shaped hut that had surprised me when I first arrived; Anna Wertz occupied a Swiss Chalet which on closer observation turned out to be a cuckoo clock. Not, of course, a cuckoo clock that really worked, but there was a lead

bird looking out of a window under the roof. The window was not a real window, actually it was modelled on the wall of the hut and did not look in or out on anything. The Marquise lived in a red toadstool with yellow spots. She had to climb a small ladder to get inside and this must have been very uncomfortable.

Maude, who I mentioned during the first teatime assembly, and who actually did make her own clothes, very cleverly I think from brown paper patterns, shared living quarters with Vera Van Tocht, in a double bungalow which must have once been a birthday cake. Originally it had been painted pink and white although these colours had not been able to resist the summer rains. There was a cement candle on the roof with a cement flame which was difficult to recognize at first because the yellow paint on the candleflame had turned dark green. I sometimes thought the birthday cake hut must have improved with time and I hoped it would never be repainted with its original colours.

Georgina Sykes occupied a circus tent, or rather a cement representation of a tent with red and white stripes. The words "lk n and njoy he ow " were painted over the door, and for a long time I thought these were some mysterious foreign words. Actually it read "Walk in and enjoy the show," but time and ivy had overgrown the words.

Natacha Gonzalez had an Eskimo's igloo.

During fine weather there were plenty of concrete benches to sit on in the garden. Not, of course, that we spent most of our time sitting about. We always had plenty to do, gardening, cooking and other occupations mostly of a domestic nature.

The place I preferred was what we called the bee pond. This was really a stagnant fountain overgrown with waterlilies and enclosed with walls prettily covered with white geraniums, rambling roses and jasmine. This secluded spot was the haunt of thousands of honey bees that zimmed all through the warm days at their business. I could sit amongst the bees for hours on end and feel happy, although why they pleased me so I cannot tell.

During the morning hours we were busy, although I noticed that Anna Wertz often lay on her deck chair outside the cuckoo

clock taking the sun. If she was not lying on her deck chair, unique of its kind at Hall, she was standing in the door of somebody's hut talking. This seemed to irritate some people but personally I became used to it.

On the afternoon of the second day, later on I lost count of time, I had a visit from Georgina Sykes. At that time I did not know her name and identified her by her height. She was much taller than anybody else and wore very stylish clothes with a certain jauntish ease I had to admire. That day, I remember, she was dressed in a long black kimono and red trousers, Chinese style. This struck me as being very elegant. Her hair was cut in a long bob and although no longer abundant was cleverly arranged over a small bald patch to give the impression of a casual pageboy coiffure. Her eyes must have been large and beautiful before the pendulous mauve flesh had gathered underneath. However they still had a rather daring expression, accentuated by mascara applied with certain inaccuracy around the eye-lids.

"There are times when this place gives me the pip," I heard Georgina say after I had applied my hearing trumpet. "The beastly Gambit Female wants me to peel potatoes and I can't possibly scrounge in the kitch' when I have just done my nails." To my surprise she also wore red nail varnish which covered most of the tops of her large bony fingers.

"I thought Mrs. Gambit was a very kindly person," I said. "She smiles so much."

"We call her Rachel Rictus," said Georgina stubbing out a cigarette on my table. "Her name is Rachel, her smile is Rictus. She is a dangerous and horrible creature."

"In what way is she dangerous?" my mind went back to the invisible crematorium. I felt anxious again. I wondered if Mrs. Gambit took upon herself the punishing of the inmates of Lightsome.

"She absolutely loathes me because of the Doctor. He is a libidinous fellow and stares and stares at me during meals, this makes Rachel Rictus squirm with fury. Of course how can I stop

her beastly husband devouring me during meals?" Georgina lit another cigarette with a loud cackle of mirth, "And he is always making excuses to get me into his boudoir for cosy talks."

All this seemed very strange. Doctor Gambit was a middle-aged man and at least forty years younger than Georgina. However one never can tell with human nature and I have had too many surprises in my time not to expect them in the general order of life.

"What particular type of medicine is the Doctor's speciality?" I asked in order not to show my surprise, which would not have been polite.

"Gambit is a kind of Sanctified Psychologist," said Georgina. "The result is Holy Reason, like Freudian table turning. Quite frightful and as phoney as Hell. If one could only get out of this dump he would cease to be important, being the only male around, you know. It is really too crashingly awful all these women. The place creeps with ovaries until one wants to scream. We might as well be living in a bee hive."

Our talk at that moment was interrupted by Mrs. Gambit who appeared in the doorway carrying a bucket of potatoes. I sincerely hoped she had not been listening to our conversation.

"There are at least two members of the community missing for the morning tasks," she said, her hand pressed to her brow, which looked agonized. "It is possible that I might do everything alone while you all sit around and gossip. Everything is possible. Still for your ultimate advantage I must not allow the habit of laziness to kill your already slim chances of saving your souls. Or what might become souls with perseverance and Work. One could hardly give this dignified title to the fickle emotions most of you use instead of an immortal Self."

With a pained smile she turned towards the kitchen regions. Georgina stuck out her tongue at the receding back. Nevertheless we got up and followed her, talking quietly about the weather.

"There will be Movements at five o'clock this afternoon in the workshop," said Mrs. Gambit over her shoulder. "Anybody who is late will forfeit her supper in the usual way."

"What are the Movements?" I asked Georgina but she merely made a hideous grimace. Mrs. Gambit heard my question and stopped, setting down the bucket of potatoes.

"You had better hear at once about the Movements," she told me. "Anyone who does not understand their Significance can never get the full meaning of Inner Christianity.

"The Movements were given to us in the past by Somebody in the Tradition. They have many meanings I am not at liberty to disclose to you yet as you have only just arrived, but I can say one of their outer meanings is the harmonious evolution of the Whole organism to different Special rhythms which I play to you on the harmonium. Do not expect to grasp the meaning of the Movements when you first begin, just start off as you would any ordinary task of the day."

I did not dare ask her if these movements were gymnastics. I felt very worried and only nodded my head several times. I had meant to nod once, looking at her with what I hoped was an intelligent expression. Somehow my head went on nodding nervously and I had a job to get it stopped.

Georgina nudged me and said something but I could not hear as I had forgotten my trumpet in the lighthouse. I had begun to like Georgina, she seemed so gay. She must have belonged to some fashionable group of people before her family found her too senile to keep at home. She must have had a very exciting and sophisticated life. I hoped she would tell me about it one day, which she did, several times over.

In the kitchen we all sat around a large scrubbed table peeling vegetables. Those who were not present must have been occupied with other work outside. Including Mrs. Gambit there were five of us. Georgina, Vera Van Tocht, Natacha Gonzalez and myself. Mrs. Van Tocht, whom I never could call by her first name, was very imposing. She was fat, so fat that her face and shoulders were almost the same width. In the midst of all this face were little puckered features, cunning eyes and pursed mouth.

Natacha Gonzalez was also on the heavy side but looked quite small compared to Mrs. Van Tocht. Natacha wore her hair in a

bun. Having Indian blood she had more hair than anybody else and we envied her. Her face was a pale lemon colour, denoting a bad liver. Her eyes were large like prunes, with heavy lids.

Everybody talked and worked at the same time but as I could not hear them I dedicated myself to cleaning French beans; French beans in this country are rather coarse and have strings on each side like ropes. We had been working for about an hour when there was a strange incident. Natacha Gonzalez poured all her vegetables and dirty water into my lap and got up with her arms raised and her eyes popping. She stood rigid for at least two minutes and collapsed into her chair. Her eyes were now closed and her head sunk on her breast.

"She hears voices," yelled Georgina in my ear. "When she does that she thinks she is getting a stigmata and starts fattening up for Easter." In spite of her fainting condition I saw Natacha's mouth tighten, as if she heard. Mrs. Van Tocht looked at Georgina angrily and got up to administer wet dish cloths to Natacha's head. Mrs. Gambit said something I could not hear but looked uninterested.

After a while the vegetable peeling was resumed. When the clock struck twelve we went out for a walk around the garden before lunch. I had to change my dress as I was soaking wet, having received a large pan full of water in my lap. I hoped not to catch cold. Anna Wertz was stretched comfortably in her deck chair and seemed to be talking to herself.

That afternoon I arrived in the workshop punctually at five o'clock for the Movements. There were chairs around the walls but the room was otherwise bare except for the harmonium. We all sat down in silence till Mrs. Gambit appeared and stood beside the harmonium. I had thoughtfully brought my trumpet so as not to miss anything. I felt very anxious.

"This afternoon we are going to begin with Primary Zero," said Mrs. Gambit passing a hand across her brow. "We have a newcomer amongst us who has no experience yet of the Work. For her benefit I will give a demonstration of Primary Zero." She paused, looked at the floor for a moment as if collecting herself,

then started to rub her stomach in a circular clockwise movement and tap the top of her head with the other hand. I felt relieved as I had done this in the nursery and did not have much difficulty repeating Mrs. Gambit's movements. After a moment's demonstration she sat down at the harmonium and applied herself to the instrument with great energy for somebody of such a delicate constitution. Not only did her arms, elbows and shoulders heave, but she actually bounced up and down on her seat, as if riding a mechanical horse. We all did the movements, changing hands every ten rounds on the stomach. It was not too strenuous but I was pleased when we stopped.

Mrs. Gambit twirled around on her seat and addressed me before I got the trumpet to my ear. "Eh? eh? eh?" I said as she repeated: "Marian Leatherby, the first movements are not Widdershins. Please watch Maude Wilkins carefully, she is familiar with most of the exercises."

We repeated the same thing four times and each time the harmonium got louder. "Now everybody get up and we will run through numbers four and five bis. Marian Leatherby kindly stand by me and watch the others, you will participate next time."

I walked over and stood by her obediently and they started what was for me impossible to follow. The only thing which was clear was that they stood on one leg like storks and wobbled dangerously. The rest was a series of jerks where arms flew out in all directions and heads twisted and turned till I thought their necks must break. Then a terrible thing happened to me. I started to laugh and could not stop. Tears poured down my face and I covered my mouth with my hand, hoping they would think I had a secret sorrow and was weeping and not laughing.

Mrs. Gambit stopped her exercise on the harmonium. "Mrs. Leatherby, if you are unable to control your emotions kindly leave the room."

I left and sat down on the nearest bench where I laughed and laughed and laughed. Of course this was irreverent behaviour but there was nothing I could do about it. Even when I was still a young woman I was occasionally overtaken by spasms of

uncontrollable laughter, always in public. Once I remember in a theatre accompanied by my friend Marlborough I had to be almost carried out because a man in a frock coat got up to recite some very dramatic poetry. Whether this was a nervous reflex or the poetry seemed to me really comic I cannot remember. Marlborough always seemed to be present when I was overtaken by my spasms, which he was pleased to call Marian's maniac laughter. He always enjoyed seeing me making an exhibition of myself. This got me wondering how Marlborough was enjoying Venice. He must be constantly floating about in a gondola, possibly accompanied by his crippled sister. Again I asked myself what could possibly be wrong with this sister that I had never even seen a snapshot of her during thirty years friendship with Marlborough? It must be something quite spectacular like having two heads. In this case he would hardly take her out in gondolas unless, perhaps, she sat behind a gauze curtain. Thick gauze, or even cheesecloth.

Marlborough comes from a rather aristocratic family so one could expect some kind of peculiarity. Although I had a mad grandmother, and my family was not aristocratic at all. But can cows be aristocrats? two-headed calves are quite common in fairs.

I was thinking all this when I was joined by Mrs. Van Tocht, who sat down ponderously. She was still breathing heavily from the exertion of the movements.

"Somebody is singing *O Sole Mio* to Marlborough who is floating around in a gondola with his two-headed sister," I said, and stopped abruptly. Really I must learn not to say my thoughts aloud. The image had been so clear that I had seen her two heads through the lemon cheesecloth curtains of the gondola. Mrs. Van Tocht ignored what I said and leaned on me in a conspiratorial fashion so that I had difficulty in adjusting my hearing trumpet.

"You may confide your life's tragedy to me," she said, puffing and panting. "We all have our trials and sorrows on the path of life till we see the light."

"I have had my difficulties," I replied with the intention of complaining about Muriel and Robert. This would have been highly agreeable, but just as I was beginning about the television

37

set she interrupted me with an impatient gesture: "Yes, I understand all. There are few dark corners in the human heart that I have not probed with my special insight. I am not a visionary like Mrs. Gonzalez, Natacha. Dear Natacha. But I have astral insight which enables me to help and comfort my fellow creatures. In my own humble way I have turned many erring souls to the light, yet my poor gifts are nothing compared to the wonderful powers of Natacha. She is controlled you understand, spiritual control is a rare and beautiful gift. Natacha is the Pure Vessel through which unseen powers are made manifest to us. 'NOT I BUT THAT WHICH WORKS WITHIN ME.' those are Natacha's constant words, she has a great limpid humility like the Master whose miracles were worked with the words 'Not I, but my father which is in Heaven.'"

During the pause I hastened to get back to Robert and the television set. "My grandson Robert," I said, "has an unpleasant addiction to television. Before he installed this horrible apparatus in the house I used to sit in the lounge after dinner and keep the whole family amused with fairy tales and anecdotes of my past life. I pride myself that I can tell a very amusing story when I wish. Nothing vulgar, of course, but witty and even spicy when I am not too troubled with my rheumatism. Rheumatism of course is a great hindrance to funny stories. Now my daughter-in-law, Muriel, is very unsympathetic to rheumatism. She is also very greedy with chocolates which she always hides, a very unpleasant habit. I often wonder how Galahad could ever manage to marry a person like Muriel. . . ."

I was beginning to enjoy myself but Mrs. Van Tocht soon stopped me talking with an imperious gesture, "You should never pride yourself on anything. Even something as trivial as a comic anecdote is a spiritual plague if used as a source of self-love. Humility is the fountain of light. Pride is a disease of the soul. Many people come to me seeking advice and spiritual comfort. When I lay my hands on them to calm their anxiety and fill them with Love and Light I always say 'First be Humble. A full cup cannot receive.'"

She was almost sitting on top of me, I could hardly breathe, yet I was determined to tell her more about Muriel: "My daughter-in-law started giving bridge parties after Robert brought the television set to the house. At least it would have been bridge, in my day. Now they call it Canasta Party. They actually turned me out of the lounge when people came in to play this ridiculous game. The first evening I refused to leave the room and told fourteen Parrot stories without forgetting the end of more than six."

I hoped that she would ask me to tell one of these stories, and I had just decided to tell her the Yorkshire Parrot story when she began again: "Wednesday evenings Natacha gives little groups in our Bungalow. I am sure you would find great spiritual profit if you joined us. There would only be Natacha, Maude, you and myself, all very cosy and intimate. Natacha gives us the Messages, sent to each one of us individually from the great unseen, and then we hold hands around a little table and exchange our vibrations. There are times when we are favoured with materializations from the astral plane."

I had only got halfway through the Parrot story when she heaved herself off the bench and said, "Then we shall expect you at eight-thirty on Wednesday evening at my bungalow. Do not mention this to Mrs. Gambit as she has great spiritual pride and is jealous of Natacha's wonderful powers. Besides we keep the Circle a secret in order to concentrate astral energy."

With these mysterious words she lumbered off, leaving me wondering how the Yorkshire Parrot story ended. Anna Wertz suddenly appeared on the path and I got up and turned towards my bungalow, pretending I had not seen her. But she walked faster than I and soon caught up with me. Anna did not really prevent me from enjoying the evening air and without my hearing trumpet her voice was a distant murmur like a crowd on a far off football field. Making no attempt to listen, I saw with delight that Venus was out and sparkled over the tree tops. I longed to tell Anna how I loved this bright planet but I knew that would be out of the question. She was looking rather cross, probably she had been working

dreadfully hard again, although I could not imagine what she did that was so exhausting.

How delightful it would be to find a few people, or even one person, unconditionally thrilled by what one had to say. I imagined telling an excited audience Parrot stories for hours on end without anyone interrupting or yawning. Or again to explain how very unfair Muriel and Robert had always been to me, and how Galahad used to have a strong character which was gradually sapped away by Muriel's nagging. Mere day dreams, one might say, yet there are people who talk a lot and nobody ever dares interrupt them. What can they possibly have to say that is so interesting? Perhaps if one had ghostly visitations like Mrs. Gonzalez it would be possible to excite interest in other people, especially if one talked to them about themselves. There, I suppose, was the secret. People only like whatever concerns themselves and I am no exception to this rule.

We all like to be popular but what a price to pay, always to talk about the other person and never about oneself. It is doubtful if one would get any enjoyment at all, unless of course one was constantly invited to tea with French pastries. Port wine might be served instead of tea if a very interesting person happened to prefer that. Especially if I was that interesting person and I only talked about other people. In that case perhaps they might consider changing beverages.

I saw myself sitting in a warm parlour with scarlet curtains surrounded by happy, confidential but vague faces. I drank glass after glass of rich Portuguese wine occasionally washed down with a tiny French eclair. Everybody got happier and happier, they burst into applause as I reached the lighthouse, Anna Wertz had disappeared. She must have noticed that I had not been paying attention to what she was telling me. Poor Anna, how terrible for her that nobody ever liked listening to her talk.

Venus sparkled over the trees and it was almost supper-time. I fancied a nice boiled egg for supper, but one had to eat whatever appeared on the table. Although Dr. Gambit allowed me to abstain

from meat I could not take two helpings of vegetables instead so I sometimes got up hungry from the table. He told us that as one grows older one needs less food, that over-eating killed old people quicker than anything else. I dare say he was right, but we old people get a lot of simple pleasure from eating.

I wondered how Dr. Gambit and Mrs. Van Tocht kept so fat on our frugal meals. I supposed they did some private eating in their rooms, though how Mrs. Van Tocht managed to get extra food was a mystery. Mrs. Gambit was always watching over the kitchen like a lynx and the storeroom was kept locked.

I decided to discuss all this with Georgina who seemed generally well informed. There was another important question I decided to discuss with Georgina, that concerned the portrait of the Nun which hung opposite my place at mealtimes. During meals Dr. Gambit would usually make long discourses on theoretical matters which I did not understand. While the doctor held forth I had plenty of time to examine the winking Nun. My interest increased as time went on. Georgina was cultured and often mentioned famous artists that had been madly in love with her. So pretending my interest was purely artistic, I questioned her about the painting.

"It might be the Zurbarán school," she said, looking uncommonly thoughtful. "Probably painted in the late eighteenth century. Spanish of course, an Italian could never have done anything so enchantingly sinister. A nun with a leer. Unknown master."

"Do you suppose she is really winking, or is she blind in one eye?" I asked, anxious for Georgina's opinion on a more personal aspect of the lady.

"She is definitely winking; the bawdy old bag is probably peeking at the monastery through a hole in the wall, watching the monks prancing around in their knickers." Georgina had a one-track mind. "It is beautiful," she added. "I wonder the Gams let it hang amongst their hideous possessions. Everything in the house ought to have been burnt long ago apart from the leering abbess."

Certainly the painting had a force all of its own and I was pleased that Georgina was also impressed. She was such a cultured person, almost an aristocrat.

Really it was strange how often the leering abbess occupied my thoughts. I even gave her a name, keeping it strictly to myself. I called her Doña Rosalinda Alvarez della Cueva, a nice long name, Spanish style. She was abbess, I imagined, of a huge Baroque convent on a lonely and barren mountain in Castile. The convent was called El Convento de Santa Barbara de Tartarus, the bearded patroness of Limbo said to play with unbaptised children in this nether region. How all these fancies occurred to me I do not know, but they kept me amused, especially during sleepless nights. Old people do not sleep much.

"Yes," said Georgina, "how those Spaniards understood the painting of black drapery. So much more superbly blackly depressing than anyone else's black. The old Lady's habit has the texture of orchid petals and the colour of Limbo. It really is a wonderful painting. Her face surrounded by that white starched frill is as luminous as the full moon, and just as bewitching." Somehow I felt that Georgina understood the painting of the leering abbess better than I ever could.

Three days after my arrival at Lightsome Hall I had my first private interview with Dr. Gambit. I was summoned to his study by a small piece of pink memorandum paper bearing this message: "Marian Leatherby kindly report to my office at six p.m. L. Gambit, Psych."

The office, or study as it was called on ordinary occasions, was situated on the ground floor of the main building. It was a small room looking out onto a circular balcony and, further on, the lawn and cyprus trees which skirted the west wing. The room was stuffed to suffocation point with bibelots and heavy furniture. Books, magazines, brass Buddhas and marble Christs, archeological miscellanea, fountain pens and all kinds of other small accessories occupied every square inch of space. Dr. Gambit sat behind a huge mahogany desk which was half as large as the room.

He looked professional as he told me to sit down. I found a free space with some difficulty.

"For weeks or even years we do not expect results from the Work," said Dr. Gambit. "We do, however, expect Effort. This Institute was founded with the intention of introducing people to the Work. Inner Christianity. We choose our initiates from people already experienced in the sorrows and difficulties of life in three dimensions, people, in fact, already so disappointed with existence that emotional ties would be weakened with time and frustration. This condition is apt to open psychic doors for New Truth."

He looked at me severely but I only kept nodding, as I do when I feel nervous. He wrote something in a notebook and then continued: "Every member of this community is closely Watched and Studied in order that they can receive Help. No Help can be of any avail if there is not collaboration and Effort on the part of the individual. Reports in your particular case show the following list of interior impurities: Greed, Insincerity, Egoism, Laziness and Vanity. At the top of the list Greed, signifying a dominating passion. You cannot overcome so many psychic deformities in a short space of time. You are not alone as victim of your degenerate habits, everyone has faults, here we seek to observe these faults and finally to dissolve them under the light of Objective Observation, Consciousness.

"The fact that You Have Been Chosen to join this community should give you enough stimulation to face your own vices bravely and seek to diminish their hold over you."

I was somewhat confounded by this discourse and I might say offended. After mumbling a bit to get my thoughts in order I said: "Doctor Gambit, you are in error if you think that anybody chose me as an initiate for your institution. I was sent here merely because my family wished to put me out of their way without having a murder on their conscience. My daughter-in-law Muriel chose your institution as the only home for senile ladies which was financially within her and my son Galahad's means. It is extremely doubtful that anybody within these walls had ever so

44

much as heard of me, so how can you possibly insinuate that I was chosen by the institution?"

"There are certain things that you must neither expect nor try to understand at the present," replied the doctor mysteriously. "Live your daily tasks with attention and Effort. Do not try to interpret Higher Planes and their mysteries before you can extricate yourself from Automatic Habit. Vice and Habit mean the same thing. As long as we are victims of Habit we are slaves to Vice. I advise you to begin by giving up cauliflower. I notice you have an inordinate appetite for this vegetable, your reigning passion, in fact, Greed."

Mrs. Gambit must have seen me steal a small branch of boiled cauliflower during the morning tasks in the kitchen. I must be more careful, I thought, nodding my head.

"I am happy and encouraged to see that you are already facing your Deficient Personality," said Dr. Gambit, "Personality is a Vampire and True Self can never emerge as long as Personality is dominant."

I wanted to say: "Yes, all that is true enough, but how can you criticize my greed when you are so much fatter than I am?" I could only mumble, however, and he seemed to think that I was asking for spiritual advice.

"Do not be discouraged," he said. "Effort is always rewarded when we have renounced Recompense. Although Greed is deeply rooted in your nature, the fact that you recognize it as a destructive growth will help you to dislodge it, like a dentist extracting a decayed tooth."

Surely anyone so fat must be at least as greedy as myself? Or was it Glandular? Fat people always say they have 'Glandular' trouble, though they always eat more than anyone else, like Muriel, constantly stuffing herself with chocolates and never sharing them with anybody.

In any case all this talk about vicious greed no doubt helped the economy of feeding senile old women. The drawers in that colossal desk of his were no doubt full of preserved fruits, sweet

biscuits, jujubes and caramels. The top drawer was reserved, I supposed, for perishable foods such as cheese sandwiches and cold roast chicken, so they wouldn't get forgotten under some account book in a bottom drawer.

"Glandular indeed!" I said aloud. "Never heard such nonsense."

To my surprise Dr. Gambit looked pleased and replied immediately: "There you have one of the most important practical bases for Self Observation. Glands and their function are one of the first proofs of Will over Matter."

"Glands yourself!" I replied, but I was so cross that my enunciation must have been worse than usual and he went right on telling me how to observe my glands. Fat Little Whippersnapper telling me about my glands!

I must have dozed off after this as the room was very warm. I woke suddenly as the door was thrown violently open. In came Natacha Gonzalez dressed like an apparition. She wore a long white nightdress and her abundant iron grey hair streamed over her shoulders. Her yellow face had two purple spots of rage on each cheek, and she pointed at Dr. Gambit like an avenging fury: "If you do not get rid of that woman," she shouted, "I shall leave the Institute tonight."

Pretending to be still asleep I put the trumpet cautiously to my left ear. Dr. Gambit stood up in some agitation and sat Mrs. Gonzalez in the nearest chair on top of a few paper-backed novels. "Be serene, Natacha, remember your Special Mission," he said, lighting a cigarette and putting it in her mouth himself. I observed all this out of one eye. I must say Dr. Gambit had a most unexpected attitude to Natacha Gonzalez.

"Dear Lady, Serenity is the Tribute you must pay to the wonderful Gifts which flow through you. Serenity Natacha," he repeated, fixing her with the two thick lenses of his spectacles. "Serenity Natacha, you are serene, perfectly blissfully calm and serene."

Mrs. Gonzalez had relaxed a bit and was now happily puffing

47

the cigarette. "You are Serene Natacha, you are quite calm and you are relaxing gently. Now tell me what you were going to say when you came in."

"It concerns a Message from The Great Beyond which was bestowed upon me by a tall bearded man." Her voice now had the quality of a sleep-talker. She still gripped the chair spasmodically, however, till the knuckles stood out white. "This Towering Bearded figure glided into my bedroom and handed me a wreath of white roses saying 'You are Natacha, upon this fount of light I build my teaching, to You I give the roses of Heaven, Your odour of Sanctity is fragrant like blossoms to the Lord. My name is Peter, which is Rock.'"

"Tell me all, Natacha, you are Serene and calm, blissfully calm and Serene," said Dr. Gambit, placing a forefinger on Natacha's forehead.

"Then the Holy man took my hand and we were gently wafted upwards and he stroked my hair saying 'Natacha these Holy Roses from the Kingdom of Heaven are the Symbol of your Work amongst men and women. You are The Pure Vessel through which the Will of the Master is made manifest to his flock. Rejoice for you are chosen to lead others, Natacha Blessed amongst women.'"

"Then," continued Natacha, gripping the chair and opening one eye, "he told me there was a message for Georgina Sykes. He said 'Tell Georgina Sykes that if she goes on spreading vicious gossip about Dr. Gambit and herself that her ever decreasing chances of Salvation will be petrified for ever."

I saw the Doctor twitch nervously. "What sort of gossip?" he asked sharply, then, modifying his tone to a hypnotic drawl, "What sort of gossip, Natacha?—you are blissfully calm and Serene—What sort of gossip?"

Natacha's voice was anything but blissfully calm and serene as she replied viciously: "You are going to get a nasty surprise about that backbiting, malignant old Trollop. Those sagging, baggy eyes of hers are going to ogle once too often."

Dr. Gambit made a slight gesture of impatience, "What sort of

gossip, Natacha? Reply, you are now relaxed and Serene, REPLY."

"She goes around the whole Institution telling people that you are trying to seduce her, and even tried to enter her bungalow at night."

"Monstrous!" exclaimed Dr. Gambit angrily, "The woman must be mad."

"Georgina Sykes is an obscene old woman," said Natacha with unction. "She is a sex maniac and ought not to be allowed to mix with the other members of the community. She warps their minds."

"I shall have to talk to her at once," said Gambit in extreme agitation. "This might ruin the reputation of the whole Institution!"

"That is not all," added Natacha. "She insulted me outrageously. Naturally I hurried to her bungalow to transmit the Message, with all the purity of mind I have cultivated for my Mission. 'Georgina,' I said gently, 'I have a message for you.' She replied very rudely, saying: 'If it's a message from heaven stuff it up your something or other.' I was shocked and pained but I maintained my Inner Radiance and I admonished her to listen to what could only be for her own good. Then she pushed me out of the place and slammed the door. Still glowing with secret peace I went about the day's toil joyfully, till I had the misfortune to meet Georgina a half an hour ago on the fuschia walk. She stopped me and hissed like an angry serpent: 'Natacha Gonzalez you are a lamentable little hypocrite and if you ever try and relay any more of your beastly messages to me I shall spit in your face.' That is an entire account of the whole affair. It is my duty to open your consciousness to the danger and perfidy of this horrible woman. I will resign from the Institution if she stays on."

Doctor Gambit seemed to have forgotten about blissful serenity. He was now pacing up and down wringing his hands saying, "This is a terrible occurrence. Georgina Sykes is kept here by her nephew, who pays twice as much as anybody else because

she takes extras. Morning Bovril, clean sheets twice a week, massage and ovaltine at bedtime. It is most distressing, Mrs. Gambit must be spared all this, her migraine would prevent me sleeping for weeks."

Natacha, who did not seem interested in these reflexions, got up to go, saying, "Take my advice and get rid of her, she is a public menace."

Finally I also got up and left. I doubt if the doctor saw me go. He was staring out of the window, looking so distressed that I felt sorry for the poor man. I noticed the doctor always seemed deflated in the presence of Mrs. Gambit, and I now understood that he was actually afraid of her. Possibly she also punished him through the stomach. The person who controls the distribution of food has almost unlimited power in a society such as ours. Mrs. Gambit's despotic rule of the kitchen seemed an unfair advantage. I wondered if it would not be possible to organize a small mutiny.

Sunday afternoon was the usual period for receiving visitors. More affectionate relatives would arrive with picnic lunches which were eaten in different corners of the garden or on the lawn. The rest of us unfavoured by this special attention would sit near the lunchers and observe them as closely as possible in order to be able to criticize them later on; subjects for discussion were always welcome. Also, people receiving sumptuous gifts such as roast chickens and chocolate cake merited close observation.

Several Sundays went past before Galahad and Muriel came to see me. They arrived towards five o'clock in the afternoon, bringing a box of multi-coloured jujubes and a letter from Carmella. I was most excited to get news of Carmella at last, but I controlled my impatience and kept the fat envelope in my pocket in order to delect it alone and unperturbed.

Muriel looked fatter than ever and Galahad, I thought, looked rather tired.

"I know you will be very happy to hear that Robert is engaged to be married," said Muriel, whose voice was always so unpleasantly loud that I was obliged to listen to her. "We are very pleased because he has chosen a nice English girl whose family are

very comfortably off. They are an old yeoman family from Devonshire. Colonel Blake was here with Flavia and the two children fell in love at the annual tennis tournament, organized by the British Club. We both think it is a most suitable match, don't we Galahad?"

Galahad said something I did not hear and Georgina walked closeby giving me a prodigious wink.

"Poor old creature," yelled Muriel at Georgina's retreating back. "She looks quite dotty. Somebody ought to give her some proper clothes."

Georgina turned her head and leered, so I knew she had heard Muriel's remark. I felt ashamed of having such an insensitive daughter-in-law. Besides, pity for Georgina was most displaced, and we all admired her elegant and rather extravagant clothes.

"So my own baby Robert is a grown up man now and taking a wife," continued Muriel in the same strident voice. "They are to be married in June. Isn't that exciting news?"

"Nothing about Robert excites me," I replied. "How are the cats? the red hen? and Rosina and her children?"

"Old Mrs. Velasquez took charge of the cats and Rosina took the red hen back to her pueblo. We had to get rid of Rosina, she became too impertinent. The house was repainted. That was Robert's idea. He wanted to invite his fiancée to a nice comfortable home. You would hardly recognize the house now. The living room is dark rose and the kitchen is seascape blue. They sell a new plastic paint which is also washable. Galahad bought some palms to stand in the vestibule and I repotted them in red lacquered tubs which I picked up 'bargain price' at the American Episcopal Jumble Sale."

Carmella had taken the cats, bless her, that was a relief. I felt less happy about the red hen. Hens in pueblos are very thin if they survive at all. Muriel went on telling me news as loud as she could. During our fifteen years cohabitation she had not talked to me half as much.

"Colonel Blake is staying over to see Robert and Flavia married. In England he is a keen sportsman and will miss the

shooting season. However he is golfing a lot and playing canasta in the evenings, so he seems to be having a lot of fun.

"Robert and Flavia are taking up amateur theatricals with the Footlight Company. They are doing a Noel Coward play which ought to be a great success. Flavia has the second most important part in the play."

The idea of Robert acting in a play gave me nausea, so I said nothing.

"Mrs. Birch," went on Muriel, "was so upset that Flavia got the part in the play that she made a public scene. Really that woman has no shame, at her age. Acting! She must be sixty at least."

The sun had started sinking when they left at last. I felt sorry for Galahad, but the day when I could have helped him was long past.

Carmella's letter crackled in my pocket, and I hurried off to read it in peace. It was really delightful to look once more on her delicate handwriting and violet coloured ink. "Dear Marian," she wrote, "I hardly know if you will read this letter even if it ever reaches you. I cannot trust that horrible Muriel to deliver it safely and even if she does you may be suffering too much to read letters.

"I have had some awful nightmares about you in that huge dreary cement building. Modern style architecture is always so depressing. Those stark exercise yards full of menacing hounds, those lantern jawed policewomen making you all tramp around in your grey uniforms. Do they make you sew sacks? I always thought that such an unprofitable occupation. Tuesday night I dreamt you escaped in a strait jacket and hopped for miles. If you can, smuggle out a short note. I should feel very much relieved as I am not sure that they don't give truth serum all the time.

"The two cats are well and happy. I did not arrive in time to save the red hen. Alas, she is almost sure to be eaten soon. The cats felt a little strange at first but they soon settled down. All cats are psychic, as you know, and they felt my sympathy immediately.

"Apart from the nightmares I have had about you I have been having recurrent dreams about a nun in a tower. She has a most interesting face, which is slightly deformed by a perpetual wink. I cannot imagine who she is. One of my correspondents, perhaps?

"I am thinking of organizing a visit to you, although if we have to talk through bars under the eye of a policewoman I shall not be able to bring you chocolate cake and a bottle of port as I wished. If possible let me know the exact measurement between each bar and I will be able to calculate what could fit through. Cigarettes are always a comfort and even the narrowest space would be wide enough to pass cigarettes. Should I bring marijuana cigarettes to alleviate your misery? Arabs, I am told, sell this herb behind the San Fandila Market. In order to buy it I would have to go armed, as it is a very dangerous and tough part of the city. Naturally I would go to any lengths to lessen your suffering, however it would be very difficult to obtain marijuana in any quantity so please be precise in your letter if you really need it.

"Planning my visit to you has been most absorbing as I have different disguises for each visit so that they do not get suspicious in case I have to help you to escape. Elisa, the new maid, tells me her grandfather has an old charro costume which was left to him by his late employer and he would be willing to hire it out for a small sum. I had rather hoped to arrive dressed as a Hungarian general but this is rather a rare uniform in these parts. A toreador costume would also be colourful, but I think this might turn out too expensive. In any case I ought not to be too elaborate as that might arouse their suspicions. A large false moustache and dark glasses are usually enough to change one's appearance considerably.

"Of course it would be much more convenient if we could communicate by means of underground passages. With this end in view I made some plans based on termite engineering, as I do not suppose we would be able to obtain machinery. I enclose the plans in this letter, please take care that they do not fall into the hands of the authorities. The consequences might be disastrous for us both. Brain Washing, they say, is the latest method of torture, thumb screws went out of fashion long ago. In case you have not heard of Brain Washing this is a form of Mental Torture provoked by constant anxiety inflicted by others. It soon drives you mad, so be careful to take no notice if they say you are to face the shooting

squad. Refuse any injections even if they say they are vitamins, it might be Truth Serum. This is the part of the brain washing which makes you swear you have done a lot of things you never even thought of doing.

"I keep dreaming that I am dead and have to bury my own corpse. This is most unpleasant as the corpse has begun to go bad and I don't know where to put it. Last night I had the same dream, the winking nun, and then the arduous duty of interring my own corpse. I had decided to have it embalmed and sent here to my house, cash on delivery. But as soon as the funeral agency arrived here I was so alarmed at having to face my dead body that I sent it back again to the funeral parlour without paying. What a relief it is that we don't really have to undertake the worry and trouble of our own burials.

"Do study the enclosed plans carefully and reply by return of post. I enclose two pesetas that you could use to bribe somebody to smuggle the letter out of the Institution. I would also need the drawing of the entire layout which you could do in secret. You draw it as if you were hovering above in a helicopter, not as an ordinary watercolour. Wouldn't it be wonderful if I won a helicopter in a crossword puzzle competition? There is not much hope though I am afraid, as they never give such practical prizes.

"Do not give up hope entirely in spite of the horror of your situation. I am mobilizing all my mental capacities to obtain your unconditional freedom.

Ever most affectionately, Carmella.

Having read Carmella's letter over several times I sat plunged in thought. The winking nun could be no other than Doña Rosalinda Alvarez Cruz della Cueva. How very mysterious that Carmella should have seen her telepathically. How excited she would be when I told her about the oil painting and how the abbess occupied my thoughts.

Carmella's plans for the underground passage between the Institution and her house seemed very difficult to realize in actual

fact. Who would do all the digging? Where would we find dynamite to explode our way through underground rocks? And with pickaxes it would take Carmella and I forever to burrow at least ten kilometres underground.

Nevertheless I decided I would make a careful plan of the Institution and send it to Carmella as soon as possible. I had not heard of anybody having any difficulty sending off correspondence and a lot of ladies received uncensored letters, so it would not be necessary to smuggle out the letter as Carmella suggested. This made everything easier. How kind of Carmella to take charge of my dear cats at her own expense. How I longed to see her again and suck violet flavoured lozenges on the porch.

It was Sunday, so supper was rather more informal than usual. Cold roast beef and potato salad were placed on the table and not passed around. Junket and buns were taken with coffee in the lounge. We did our own washing up in relays, as the maids were out that day. An hour of quiet recreation was allowed after this meal. Some of us talked, knitted or played simple games. The Marquise Claude la Checherelle and Maude always played snakes and ladders after supper. It was a ritual which I liked to watch. The Marquise always moved her square with military strategy, giving us lurid accounts of battles she had fought and won all over Europe and Africa. Maude, who was timid, hardly ever dared interrupt these repetitive wartime souvenirs.

"The mud was up to our necks," the Marquise would say, tossing the dice on the board. "The Captain and I had bullets whizzing through our caps as we peeped over the trenches. The Germans were pressing forward mercilessly with their heavy artillery. Tanks chattered their machine guns like avenging robots. The situation was desperate. We were mortally tired, yet duty kept us staggering at our posts. 'The only hope is direct attack, *mon capitaine*, we are under fire on both flanks.' The captain's strong jaw tightened perceptibly, 'It would be cold blooded murder for the troops,' he replied looking through his mudcaked face with sharp blue eyes. I gripped his arm and pointed at the sea behind us, 'Where shall we retreat?' I said, my voice

husky with emotion. 'Should we not rather die fighting than be squashed into the mud by the tanks?' 'As usual I must bow to your advice' said the Captain, *'en avant!'*

"And that's how the battle of Ypres turned out in our favour," continued the Marquise modestly. "Most of us were wiped out, some of us drowned trying to swim the channel to Dover. Our little batallion forced the German tanks to retreat after twenty-four hours of constant fire."

At that moment Maude threw a six and her square climbed up a ladder almost to victory. The Marquise swore under her breath and threw a two which got her nowhere. "I never am lucky on Sundays," she said. "I was born on a Tuesday. If one could consider that lucky. But I do not complain, for my life has been full of excitement and pleasure. For instance I remember how we escaped the German snipers in North Africa. It was a forced march through barren mountainous country. I was second in command of our batallion. We were escorting two red cross ambulances to the desert...."

"I am afraid I have won," said Maude timidly. "Pure luck of course. This game requires no real skill like chess."

"So you have," said the Marquise, peering closely at the Snakes and Ladders. "Well I believe a sporting instinct is more important than always winning, so let me congratulate you warmly. Of course I might have won if it had not been Sunday."

Mrs. Gambit rang a small bell. We all rose to retire to our respective villas. I was thankful that I lived in a lookout and not in a cement toadstool like the Marquise, although she never complained about climbing up a ladder every time she wanted to get into bed. It must have reminded her of the happy days when she was climbing in and out of shell holes.

The moon was almost full and lighted our way through the garden. I walked with Maude back to the double bungalow she occupied with Mrs. Van Tocht.

"Moonlight always makes me think of Switzerland," said Maude sadly. "As a girl I used to go to Mürren for the winter sports. I never was much good at skiing although I could skate a

bit. Not figure skating or anything fancy, just ordinary getting along."

"Yes indeed," I replied. "There is nothing I love so much as snow lit by moonlight. For years I have wanted to go to Lapland just to be able to sail along in a sledge drawn by those white woolly dogs and admire the snow. Further North they use reindeer which also give milk. I suppose they make cheese too, although I fancy it might have a rather goaty taste which never appealed to me."

"We really must not allow ourselves to become victims to daydreaming," said Maude. "Dr. Gambit says daydreaming saps more energy than riding a bicycle. I am sure he must be right, although I am not clever enough to understand the reasons for all he tells us. Still, at our age it is difficult not to indulge a little in small pleasures. Although I know you will think I am silly, I sometimes find myself imagining that I am strolling through a whispering birch forest somewhere in the North. It is early spring and the last frosts make the grass crackle under my feet."

"Yes I know," I said fervently. "Birch trees, silver birch that seem so much more alive than these nasty palm trees."

"It is so vivid," went on Maude, "that it makes up a whole story. Would you mind very much if I told you about it?"

"I would enjoy hearing about it very much," I replied, hoping it would not take too long, as I wanted to begin a letter to Carmella before it got too late. Mrs. Gambit insisted that all lights be extinguished by eleven o'clock.

"Well," said Maude, "there I am dressed in tweed trousers, leather jacket and strong brogue shoes; I am strolling alone whistling, or rather humming. I cannot whistle since I lost my teeth. The birch forest is full of babbling brooks which I cross on smooth stepping stones. These are sometimes rather slippery and I have to steady myself with a stout bramble walking stick I always carry. Such clear frolicking little brooks. They seem to promise all kinds of innocent fun! A light wind rustles the leaves of the birch trees, the air is fresh and cool. As I stroll along I become aware that I have a purpose, and soon with a thrill of joy I know what it is. I must find a magic cup, hidden somewhere in the wood. Then I

57

come upon a marble statue of Diana and her dogs. She is half-covered with moss, and strides perpetually through the forest. The cup lies at the foot of the statue. It is a silver chalice brimming over with golden honey. I sip the honey and return the cup to Diana with a thankful prayer, or rather it is not quite like that. I make an attempt to sip the honey but it is too thick and I have to look around for a spoon. There are no spoons so after licking the rim of the chalice I return it still nearly full of honey to the Goddess, and then I say my prayer of Thanks.

"The statue of Diana is not far behind and I find a small iron key lying half hidden under a stone. I know I shall need this so I put it in my pocket. Sure enough I suddenly find myself in front of a wooden door imbedded in a mossy wall. Just as I am wondering if I ought to open it or not and I am trying the iron key in the lock somebody creeps up behind me and roughly pushes me through the door. The door opens of its own accord and I fall into a strange luxurious bedroom furnished in a style which seems Renaissance. But I am so ignorant about art that it might easily be gothic or even baroque. The fourposter bed is occupied by a woman wearing a frilly white nightcap. She is winking at me and I recognize her as the nun in the oil painting that hangs in the dining room."

"Very strange indeed," I said. "That painting has occupied my thoughts since I first saw it. Who is the nun?"

"Nobody seems to know," said Maude. "Or rather they pretend they do not know although I often think that Christabel Burns could tell a lot if she wished. She is such a secretive person though and never talks much to anybody."

"Perhaps she feels different being a Negress," I said. "Negresses have different sorts of souvenirs from us. I often wanted to talk to her but she always seems too busy."

"Well I suppose I ought to hurry to bed," said Maude. "I share a bungalow with Mrs. Van Tocht. You know, Vera. She doesn't like me to go to bed late as she says she can hear me taking my shoes off through the walls. She is a very light sleeper. I do appreciate Vera so much. She is very spiritual. I could never reach her higher plane, I am afraid."

"Yes, she tells me you have seances on Wednesday evenings."
Maude looked a little surprised. "She told you?" she said. "That
means she must think you have possibilities of Initiation. I do hope
you will join us on Wednesday?"

"Thank you," I replied. "I would be very happy." I thought
perhaps they served light refreshments, possibly liqueurs.
Somebody had told me that Mrs. Van Tocht had private means.
Something must have kept her fat.

"What about Natacha Gonzalez?" I asked. "They say she has
supernatural powers." There was a slight hesitation before Maude
replied, "Yes she is a very spiritual person too. She has visions.
Goodnight, I really must go before Vera gets into bed."

She left me wondering why she looked so fearful when I
mentioned Natacha Gonzalez. The moon floated high in the
heavens. I began to compose my letter to Carmella. It really was a
pity that she was not present to enjoy so much mystery. I thought
of suggesting that she should come for a weekend, providing I
could obtain permission from Mrs. Gambit. Carmella would have
some very interesting theories about all these people. Before
retiring into the Lookout I stood outside admiring the moon and
stars and listening to the night creatures through my trumpet.
Anna Wertz was talking to herself in the distance, a cricket
chirped and a nightingale sang nearby. Now where, I wondered,
had I put my pen and ink? The paper, I knew, was in the closet
upstairs.

When I had written Carmella all the news I could think of I
went to bed, leaving the rest for another day. The moon shone in
through my window and I could not get off to sleep, but lay half
dreaming and half awake, a state which is quite familiar to me
now. Souvenirs from the far past rose like bubbles in my mind and
things I thought were long forgotten came back as clear as if they
had just happened.

The Luxembourg Gardens and the smell of chestnut trees, Paris.
St. Germain des Prés, having breakfast on the terrace of a cafe
with Simon, whose face was as clear and solid as if still full of life,
but Simon must be dead for thirty years now, there is nothing left

of him as far as I know. Simon talking like the Arabian Nights, Love and Magic. Then I dreamt that I was preparing lunch in a summer house in the hollow of a large garden with Simon. There was something important I had to ask him and I touched his chest. "But you are as solid as I am." I told him, "O Simon why did you die before you could tell me what it is all about? Simon, what is it like being dead?" That was what I had to ask him and I felt embarrassed, he looked puzzled for a moment then he said:

"You think it is going to end all the time but it never does." He had beautiful eyes like a Siamese cat. Simon lost in interminable twilight gardens, never getting free, and he knew so much. Simon. Perhaps I would still be in Paris, oh the joy if I could just walk along the quais and admire the books, or look at the Seine from the Pont Neuf. I would walk up rue St. André des Arts to the market and buy red wine and brie for lunch, that would be plenty for my frugal needs. Pierre, rue des Beaux Arts. Clever Pierre with all his wonderful theories coming to such a sad end. He was drowned in his bath, murdered they say, by a still life painter. Pierre had flown into a rage because he recognized a carrot in one of the paintings of the murderer, Jean Prissard. The outraged artist had crept into Pierre's apartment and, finding him in the bath, held him under water till he expired. Poor Pierre, I forget if his murderer was sent to the guillotine. Pierre who was so wonderfully clever and sensitive about painting that if a canvas had anything but one colour painted on the same colour he would almost faint with horror. Form, he said, was outdated and vulgar. Therefore the carrot, which may not have been a carrot at all, sent him to an untimely death.

Monday or Tuesday, I forget which, I was sitting by the bee pond trying to teach myself to crochet. Mrs. Gambit said idleness was the real cause of my terrible greed, so I thought I would try and crochet a scarf. Maude had given me some green wool and a crochet lesson. It was not nearly as simple as she would have me believe. I had stopped to admire the bees and envy them such

efficient industry, when Natacha Gonzalez appeared suddenly. Her head was wrapped in a mauve scarf as if she had toothache.

"I am entirely exhausted," she said, rolling her eyes like huge revolving prunes. "Impossible to get any sleep for three days."

"Perhaps Mrs. Gambit would give you some Sedebrol if you asked her. I believe it is very effective," I said kindly. Natacha clasped her head and groaned. "Sedebrol! but of course you do not understand. I am dizzy with sleep, only I dare not close my eyes because of the rats."

This gave me a shock, I was always terrified of rats and mice. "How dreadful," I said, "are there rats in your bungalow?"

"ENORMOUS rats," said Natacha. "I would say these rats are almost as big as spaniels. So of course I dare not sleep. They might gnaw off my nose."

"How horrible," I said nervously. "Mrs. Gambit ought to keep cats. She could keep a dozen cats here quite comfortably and they are such beautiful creatures. Rats and mice can't even stand the smell of cats."

"Mrs. Gambit has an allergy to cats," said Natacha. "They give her pimples."

"What nonsense!" I exclaimed, "There is nothing so clean as a healthy pussy. When I was at home I wouldn't have slept without my cats for anything."

"Mrs. Gambit," said Natacha emphatically, "Would not touch a cat to save her life. She wouldn't have a cat near the place. There is no other remedy but rat poison. I shall ask her to buy me some packets of 'Last Supper' rat poisoning. It is the most virulent and they die almost at once."

"If they are really as big as spaniels and die under the floor boards you will be stunk out of your bungalow in no time."

"I will sacrifice myself to get rid of such frightful creatures," said Natacha. "Besides, it is better to smell them than have my nose gnawed off."

"Not that I want to interrupt," said Georgina poking her head around the jasmine bush, "but I haven't seen a mouse or rat since I arrived here ten years ago."

"Vipress!" exclaimed Natacha. "I advise you not to talk to Georgina Sykes. She is a dangerous, immoral and malignant woman!" Wrapping her mauve gauze scarf tightly around her lower jaw she pointed a short forefinger at the jasmine bush. "Vipress!" she hissed through the scarf. "Poisonous reptile!" She took herself off still vituperating.

Georgina sauntered into the close and sat down. "Objectively speaking," she said, "Natacha Gonzalez stinks. I have my own little pet name for Natacha. I call her Saint Rasputina. All that tale about the rats was absolute poppycock, she was lying. Rasputina would sell her mother to the white slave traders to get a bit of publicity. She has a power complex like Hitler. She invents rats as big as spaniels just as she invents cosy chats with saints as tall as telegraph poles. It all comes to the same thing, power and more power. It is a jolly good thing for humanity that she is shut up in a home for senile females."

"I hope you are right about there being no rats here," I replied, "I have always been afraid of rats and mice, although I believe I am fond of most animals."

Georgina suddenly stared curiously at my crochet scarf, "Talking of animals, is that a jerkin for a grass snake you are knitting?" Georgina could hardly be expected to guess it was a scarf. Still it was obvious that I was doing crochet work, not knitting.

"No." I said slightly nettled. "It is not."

"Where did you get such nauseatingly green wool? It makes my dentures chatter."

"There are times when you are far too critical, Georgina. Maude Somers very kindly made me the present of this nice green wool, and I think it has a pleasant springtime colour, like early chestnut leaves."

"I hope you don't intend to wear it eventually?" said Georgina, ignoring my reproach. "You would look like Noah after he was drowned in the flood. Green is not your colour, you are far too green as it is."

"Surely you don't expect me to look like a debutante?" I asked.

"Besides Noah was not supposed to have drowned. He had an ark, you know, full of animals."

"Everybody knows that the whole bible is inaccurate. True, Noah did go off in an ark, but he got drunk and fell overboard. Mrs. Noah went aft and watched him drown, she didn't do anything about it because she inherited all those cattle. People in the bible were very sordid and a lot of cattle in those days were like a bank account."

Georgina got up and threw her cigarette end into the bee pond, it fizzled unpleasantly.

"Where are you going?" I asked, as I always enjoyed Georgina's conversation.

"I am going to read a novel so you can go on knitting your beastly sock." She stalked off with a certain creaking elegance, leaving a faint scent behind her which reminded me of rue de la Paix.

A postcard arrived for me by the evening post. It was a colourful picture of the Welsh Guards and a goat marching into Buckingham Palace.

"Madame in fine mettle. We watched the croquet finals yesterday. Very exciting match. Both rather tired. Madame sends her regards. Hoping this finds you as it leaves us in g. health. Yours Truly B. Margrave."

Margrave was most kind the way he kept me informed of Mother's health. Taking an interest in sport at the age of a hundred and ten was really admirable, but then Mother's life had been a great deal easier than my own. Ever since she left Ireland at the age of eighteen Mother had lived a constant round of dizzy pleasure. Cricket matches, shooting parties, jumble sales, shopping in Regent Street, bridge parties and face massage at Madame Pomeroy's, an unfashionable beauty parlour just off Piccadilly Circus. The fact that Mother never quite caught up with fashion was part of her charm. We always arrived too early or too late for everything. Arriving in Biarritz, I remember, in a snowstorm in the month of February. Mother took the weather as a personal insult, she believed the Riviera was on the equator, snowfall in

Biarritz convinced her that the poles were changing places and the earth was falling out of its orbit. We were the only clients in a hotel as big as Victoria Station. "No wonder people never come to Biarritz," said my Mother. "It is empty. We will go to Torquay next year, it is much cheaper and the weather is a great deal milder."

We went on to Monte Carlo where Mother found her spiritual home in the casino. She forgot about the weather. I had a flirtation with the clerk in a travel agency. He sold us tickets to Taormina and off we went to Sicily. More romance in Taormina with a head waiter called Dante. He sold us a very cheap painting by Fra Angelico which did not turn out to be authentic and was therefore not as cheap as we thought. But the weather was now beautiful and the bugumbilias in full bloom.

Back we went to Rome and admired Italian officers with hats like coal scuttles and gorgeous blue cloaks.

We drove out to the catacombs in a barouche. We trudged around Saint Peter's and admired Michelangelo's Dome. Mother was now satiated with art and decided we must go to Paris and buy clothes. "Parisian clothes," said Mother, "are famous all over the world." So we arrived in Paris and went shopping in Au Printemps. Mother was disappointed, she wanted to buy brown satin knickers but they were nowhere to be found. "We might just as well be in London," said Mother, who bought a sailor hat which didn't really suit her. "I could find all the same things in Regent Street at half the price."

We went to the Folies Bergère as Mother thought I was now old enough to see Mistinguette. "All those naked women bore me, the Greeks did it years ago," said Mother who was still annoyed about the brown satin knickers. The following evening we went to the Bal Tabarin which we both enjoyed. I danced with a very pleasant Armenian who telephoned me next day at the hotel. Mother bought tickets back to London and we left Paris before the Armenian got the chance to sell us anything.

Back in Lancashire I got an attack of claustrophobia and tried to convince Mother to let me go and study painting in London. She

thought this was a very idle and silly idea and gave me a lecture about artists. "There is nothing wrong about painting," she told me. "I paint boxes myself for jumble sales. There is a difference though in being artistic and in actually being an artist. Your Aunt Edgeworth wrote novels and was very friendly with Sir Walter Scott but she would never have called herself 'an artist.' It wouldn't have been nice. Artists are immoral, they live together in attics, you could never get used to an attic after all the luxury and comfort you have here. Besides what is there to prevent you painting at home, there are all sorts of picturesque nooks which would be delightful to paint."

"I want to paint nude models," I said. "You can't get nude models here."

"Why not?" replied Mother with a flash of logic. "People are nude everywhere if they haven't got any clothes on." Finally I did go to London to study art and had a love affair with an Egyptian. A pity I never actually got to Egypt but thanks to my Mother I did see most of Europe during my youth.

Art in London didn't seem quite modern enough and I began to want to study in Paris where the Surrealists were in full cry. Surrealism is no longer considered modern today and almost every village rectory and girl's school have surrealist pictures hanging on their walls. Even Buckingham Palace has a large reproduction of Magritte's famous slice of ham with an eye peering out. It hangs, I believe, in the throne room. Times do change indeed. The Royal Academy recently gave a retrospective exhibition of Dada art and they decorated the gallery like a public lavatory. In my day people in London would have been shocked. Today the Lord Mayor opened the exhibition with a long speech about twentieth century masters and the Queen Mother hung a wreath of gladiola on a piece of sculpture called "Navel" by Hans Arp.

How my mind runs on, or rather backwards, I shall never get on with my narrative if I can't control those memories, there are too many of them. Well, as I said before, I can't actually remember the day of the week the following events took place. It may have been

Monday or Tuesday. Wednesday, Thursday or Friday are not impossible. I do not believe it was on a Sunday. However it all started about the period I received the postcard from Margrave.

I was looking through the kitchen window in an offhand way, wondering if perhaps there was nobody about and hoping to pick up a snack.

Unfortunately, Mrs. Gambit was sitting in the kitchen shelling peas. One thing, however, struck me as most peculiar. Mrs. Gambit was sitting with a large yellow tom cat on her knees which she was stroking tenderly. Now anyone with an innate horror of cats does not let them sit on their lap, even less address them in terms of endearment. All Natacha had said about rats and Mrs. Gambit came back to my mind. Full of curiosity I walked into the kitchen and offered to help shell the peas.

"Sit down," said Mrs. Gambit. "I am pleased to see that you are struggling against idleness."

"That is a fine tom cat," I said to Mrs. Gambit. "A lot of people dislike cats, although I prefer them to almost any other pet."

"I love cats," said Mrs. Gambit. "Dear Tom always sleeps on the end of my bed as if he would like to cure my sick headaches. He is nearly always in my room, though, because cats often wander off if they are given too much liberty."

"That must be why I didn't see him before," I said. "Do let me hold him a while, it is so long since I stroked a cat."

Mrs. Gambit thought, no doubt, that I was getting too familiar, so she changed the subject of the conversation. "We have cooking classes once a week," she said. "People can practice self-control by making sweetmeats for everyone else, without tasting any of their own cooking."

To me this seemed positively sadistic, but of course I did not dare tell Mrs. Gambit my real opinion. I merely asked if we used recipes or did, so to speak, creative cooking.

"People are at liberty to cook anything they like. Of course the ingredients count as extras, so in consideration of your families we do not go in for anything extravagant. Some people use cook books

although personally I think it is preferable to make things from memory, it prevents rusty minds. All Effort is useful in the Work."

"I used to be able to make some very tasty dishes, French Cooking you know, although pastry baking was never my strong point."

"Pretension in the kitchen is no better than pretension in the drawing room," replied Mrs. Gambit. "Besides your family have not shown any desire to pay extras. Our cooking budget is far too high to allow gifts of expensive food stuff merely for the sake of showing off your capacities."

Here Mrs. Gambit gave me her agonized smile and I considered myself dismissed.

I left the kitchen feeling frustrated, without being able to stroke the tom cat.

The cooking classes started shortly after this incident and that is how Natacha came to be making chocolate fudge one afternoon. The fudge was already cool when Fate saw fit to send Mrs. Gambit a visitor. She hurried off to the drawing room leaving Natacha and Mrs. Van Tocht alone in the kitchen. Actually I was not taking part in the fudge making, I was merely an interested spectator standing outside the convenient kitchen window.

Natacha said something to Mrs. Van Tocht, who went over to the door and looked out. They could not see me as a fuschia bush made me invisible from the door. She joined Natacha again at the table and nodded. Natacha took a nail file from her pocket and drilled holes in about half-a-dozen cubes of fudge, then she opened a packet and emptied the contents into each portion of the hollowed-out sweetmeat. Then both ladies warmed the scooped out fragments of fudge in a saucepan and poured the liquid over the holes as if they had never existed. The whole process did not take long and they seemed to be in a hurry. Natacha wrapped the fudge full of the packet contents in a piece of wax paper and hurried out of the kitchen saying something to Mrs. Van Tocht who nodded again and gave a tight smile.

I crouched near the wall so that Natacha did not see me as she

walked quickly past. A second later Maude extricated herself from
behind the honeysuckle opposite me and stalked after Natacha.
Now Maude could not possibly have witnessed the strange scene in
the kitchen so I had to suppose her reasons for lurking in this region
were much the same as mine. I let both Maude and Natacha get a
start and then I took a short cut which led me behind Natacha's
igloo, where a low grill afforded a good view inside. Natacha
entered the igloo, put the fudge in the top drawer of a chest of
drawers and covered it with what looked like underclothing. She
had her back to the door so she could not see Maude who poked her
head in and watched the whole proceeding, then disappeared
before Natacha had time to turn around. I was able to follow
Natacha back to the kitchen without being seen by way of the bee
pond. As I was armed with my hearing trumpet I could overhear
the following conversation near the fuschia bush: "Well! hello
Georgina, I am so glad to have the opportunity of a word with you
alone," came Natacha's voice. "We mustn't go on snubbing each
other like two silly girls." Georgina grunted and mumbled
something I couldn't catch. Natacha replied with a sort of giggle:
"I've been playing truant and hidden some fudge in my
bungalow," she told Georgina. "I thought I would invite you to a
little feast so that we can kiss and forget about our past
difficulties."

"All right," said Georgina. "As long as we don't have to kiss.
What you have might be catching."

"Ha Ha Ha!" Natacha laughed merrily. "You have a real
English sense of humour, Georgina." All this was most surprising.
I strained my trumpet so as not to miss anything.

"Sorry I can't return the compliment," said Georgina. "You see
too many Saints."

"Perhaps I take my gifts too seriously. One never knows when
they might be withdrawn. You, Georgina, may be the next to hear
Holy Voices."

"God Forbid," said Georgina fervently.

"Well I really must get back before Mrs. Gambit notices my
absence," said Natacha. "Tonight I shall creep into your gay little

tent and bring something nice to eat. *A toute à l'heure*, Georgina!"
They separated. I heard Natacha give a happy laugh while
Georgina, walking off in the other direction, seemed to be uttering
some sort of profanity.

I walked back to Lookout very pensively, wishing that Carmella
was there to discuss all these strange events. I passed near
Natacha's igloo just in time to see a figure slip out of the door and
disappear into the garden. Maude's dainty blue muslin blouse was
unmistakeable. She had obviously been at the hidden fudge.

Although I did not feel too happy about the whole business I
cannot say that I was actually alarmed. My mind works too slowly
to jump to conclusions and when I did actually understand
everything it was too late. In the meantime a meeting with
Christabel Burns took my mind away from the fudge, so I think
that I am not entirely to blame for not warning poor Maude in
time.

Now if Christabel Burns had not been a Negress I might never
have noticed her constant, silent activity. A Negress, however, was
so exotic amongst us that one could not help finding her romantic.
Many of us had tried to draw her into conversation but she was
always too busy, carrying covered trays to and from the tower, or
sometimes bath towels and other linen. These constant journeys to
and fro made me compare Christabel to a solitary hurrying ant,
especially as she had a large posterior and very thin arms and legs.
On this particular occasion, however, Christabel was not carrying
anything, she was actually sitting on a bench near Lookout with
her hands folded neatly in her lap.

"Good evening, Mrs. Leatherby," she said with her elegant
Oxford accent. She came from Jamaica and her father had been an
eminent chemist, I learnt later.

"Good evening Mrs. Burns. How nice to see you take a rest for a
change."

"I was waiting for you, Mrs. Leatherby," she said. "The time
has come that we must have a little talk."

"Delighted, Mrs. Burns," I replied sitting down beside her. "I
have often wanted to talk to you but you always seem to be so
busy."

"The time was not ripe," replied Christabel. "It was necessary that you should first take full stock of your surroundings. Are you happy here Mrs. Leatherby?" This was a difficult question to answer as I had ceased thinking in terms of happiness for some time. I said so.

"You are really quite wrong," she said. "Happiness has got nothing to do with age. It depends on capacity. I am exactly twice your age and I may say that I am very happy indeed." I added up ninety-two and ninety-two; Christabel claimed to be one hundred and eighty-four. This hardly seemed probable but I didn't like to contradict her.

"So you see," she continued, "happiness is not reserved for young people. There is nobody that can make you happy, you must take care of this matter yourself.

"However, Mrs. Leatherby, I do not envisage an abstract discussion. I will come straight to the point. Why are you so inordinately interested in the oil painting in the dining room?" I was so taken aback by her question that I took quite some time to get my mind in order and I did a lot of mumbling. Christabel waited patiently. Finally I said: "Since the painting is hanging exactly in front of me in the dining room, and since the helpings of food allowed by Mrs. Gambit are so small I manage to finish them immediately, I have plenty of leisure to contemplate it."

"That is hardly an explanation," said Christabel, "because sitting exactly in front of you and much nearer and larger than the painting is Mrs. Van Tocht. Why do you not contemplate Mrs. Van Tocht?"

"I prefer to look at the painting. Also it would be rude if I sat and stared at Mrs. Van Tocht all during meals. Besides I am very interested in the nun represented in the painting, you can't possibly object to that?"

"Of course I do not object, Mrs. Leatherby. You must excuse my abrupt questions, they are by no means intended to be aggressive."

"Well since you ask," I said, "I find the Winking Nun has a most peculiar and indescribable expression on her face. This keeps me wondering who she was, where she came from, why she

71

perpetually winks and so on. In fact I think about her so often that she has become quite an old friend, an imaginary friend, of course."

"So you feel she is your friend? you feel she is sympathetic?"

"Yes, I think I can quite definitely say I find her friendly, although of course one would not expect much sentimentality in such a relationship." As I spoke Christabel was watching me closely, expectantly.

"Giving her a name is an evocation," said the Negress. "You must be careful how you call her."

"As a matter of fact I call her Doña Rosalinda Alvarez Cruz della Cueva. She looks so Spanish you know."

"That was her name during the eighteenth century," said Christabel. "But she has many many other names. She also enjoys different nationalities. However we will not discuss that now. What I actually came for was to bring you a little book. I know you do not enjoy reading. This will be different."

The book was bound in black leather. On the title page I read, "Doña Rosalinda della Cueva, Abbess of the Convent of Santa Barbara of Tartarus. Canonized in Rome 1756. A true and faithful rendering of the life of Rosalinda Alvarez."

"That is most extraordinary," I told Christabel. "Really, how could I possibly know her name when I am sure I never heard it?"

"Undoubtedly you must have read her name somewhere. It is written nine hundred and twenty times throughout the building, it would be extraordinary indeed if you had missed reading it."

The first page of the little book was decorated with a motive of pomegranate leaves and swords. The paper was buff coloured with age. The large old-fashioned printing was easy enough for me to read.

"I must leave you now," said Christabel, rising. "I have certain duties to perform before Venus sets. We will talk again when you have read this little volume. Please do not mention the fact this book is in your possession. The consequences might be very awkward, in ways I can not clarify at the present."

Venus already sparkled over the tower when I found myself

alone. It was evening the whole interview with Christabel Burns had been inexplicably invigorating. As I was about to enter the Lookout and start reading about Doña Rosalinda a shady figure caught my eye. Although I could not be altogether sure, I thought I saw a young man with what looked like a large bundle on his back, slipping quietly and rapidly from tree to tree.

He appeared to be taking precautions to avoid discovery. A thief perhaps? a lover of one of the servants? The latter seemed most probable, so I did not trouble to start an alarm. The servant's love life was no business of mine. If it were a thief, none of us had much to lose. I went inside the Lookout and sat down at the table and opened the book.

"A true and faithful rendering of the life of Rosalinda Alvarez della Cueva, Abbess of the Convent of Saint Barbara of Tartarus. Translated from the original Latin text by Friar Jeremias Nacob of The Order of The Holy Coffin.

"A Rose is a secret, a beautiful Rose is a Great Lady's Secret, a Cross is the parting or the joining of the Ways, this is the meaning of Abbess Rosalinda Alvarez Cruz della Cueva's name. The canonization of the Abbess was performed after certain extraordinary events witnessed by reliable dignitaries of the Church before and after her death in the year of Our Lord Jesus Christ, 1733 in the month of July. She was buried in the crypt of the Convent of Saint Barbara of Tartarus with the ceremonies and benediction of Our Mother the Holy Catholic Church. *Ab eo, quod nigram caudam habet abstine, terrestrium eoim deorum est.*

"The canonization of the Abbess sealed her sanctity with the authority of Rome; nevertheless her tomb became a sanctuary long before the Canonization. Common people made pilgrimages from afar with offerings of fruit, flowers and even cattle. These were agglomerated in the crypt.

"With a cruelly divided heart I watched the simple devotion of the peasants while I prayed long and fervently that God would grant me the necessary valour to write the whole truth about this wonderful and terrible woman.

"This document was written originally for the private perusal

of The Holy Father himself, The Pope. The result however of this presentation exceeded my wildest and most horrible nightmares. Expulsion from Holy Orders was the result of my zeal to fulfill the will of God by opening my heart and thus releasing the heavy burden within. The sacred seal of the confessional therefore no longer prevents the printing of this document; I have ceased to be a priest.

"As the once private confessor of the Abbess I believe to possess unparalleled knowledge of the workings of her dark soul.

"Further digressions on my own behalf will be unnecessary.

"The birthplace of Doña Rosalinda Alvarez Cruz della Cueva is somewhat doubtful. No definite proof exists that she was born on Spanish soil. Some hold that she came across the ocean from Egypt, some say she was born amongst the gypsies of Andalucia, others say she came across the Pyrenees from the North. The earliest evidence of her presence in Spain is a letter dated 1710, written in Madrid and addressed to the Bishop of Trève les Frêles in Provence near the city of Avignon.

"The letter concerns the opening of a tomb in Nineveh said to be the last resting place of Mary Magdalen.

"Doña Rosalinda addresses the Bishop informally, indicating a friendship of some intimacy. Probably the letter in question was written shortly after she entered the cloisters of Santa Barbara de Tartarus as a novice.

"Amongst other accusations I was held guilty of forging this document to willfully desecrate the name of Doña Rosalinda. God is my witness that this was not so.

"The handwriting composing the letter could never have issued from any other hand than that of Doña Rosalinda. Moreover her own personal seal of Crossed Swords and Pomegranates was deeply engraved at the beginning and end of the letter. Here I must insert an arbitrary extract from Rosalinda's letter which will no doubt become more comprehensible after I have related certain events later in her life.

"The extract from Doña Rosalinda's letter to the Bishop reads as follows:

'So, Mon Gros Pigeon, understand that it is imperative that you dispatch a courier immediately to Nineveh that he should barter for the precious liquid. Lose no time as interest has already been quickened in certain quarters in England. The tomb is no doubt the genuine burial ground of Mary Magdalen; the ointment which was found on the left side of the mummy may very well release secrets which would not only discredit all the gospels but which would crown all the arduous work we have shared during recent years. What do you say to that, My Fat Wildboar? After some discussion the Jew I mentioned was finally persuaded to exchange a copy of the text written on the wrappings of the mummy for a small coffer of slightly blemished pearls. By the Will of Our Great Mother the writing happened to be in Greek and as you well know I had no great task to read this script. You may imagine the transports of delight which overcame me when I learnt that Magdalen had been a high initiate of the mysteries of the Goddess but had been executed for the sacrilege of selling certain secrets of her cult to Jesus of Nazareth. This of course would explain the miracles which have puzzled us for so long. The properties of the ointment were carefully enumerated though the exact recipe for mixing this elixir was most unfortunately omitted. No doubt the precious ointment had been buried with the mummy with all Magdalen's personal riches.

" 'The secret nature of the text forbids me to send you a copy by the hazards of a courier as it might fall into the hands of Enemies. News will take some time to travel from Nineveh and by then I devoutly hope the contents of the tomb will be safely in our possession. Do not tarry over this most essential matter and hasten to dispatch trusted servants to Nineveh. Should it be in any way possible to make the journey yourself do not hesitate to leave at once taking whatever barter you see fit.

" 'In the meantime I am ingratiating myself with the lady abbess of the convent in order to precipitate my power over the other nuns. My long meditations and devotional exercises have already impressed her favourably, it will not be very long before I take my final vows. How heartily you will laugh when you read this! We

will soon be undermining the Vatican itself! My position here is not sufficiently stabilized to send for my books and I chafe cruelly at hours of precious study wasted in church, however the Ancient Art also claims its price and for my part I feel I am putting gold in the coffers each dreary hour spent kneeling on the hard stone floor.

" 'So my dear Rampant Wildpig, think of me at each meal eating black bread and drinking water whenever you want to eat a dozen pheasant pastries too many and fall under the table glutted; this would be excellent to control the growth of your great belly which will certainly kill you before your time. I also advise the seduction of less adolescents for you may wear out your sap and become a dotard before you are a magician.

" 'Now with Your Grace's permission I shall give a short account of the small failings of our lady Abbess so that you might eject the poison from your system with some hearty mirth...."

"Doña Rosalinda then exposes some irreverent anecdotes which are so offensive to a Christian mind that I refrain from putting them down here.

"The convent of Santa Barbara was at that time under the direction of the Abbess Doña Clemencia Valdez de Flores Trimestres. This venerable lady was from an excellent old Castillian family renowned as stalwart supporters of the Church and honoured by Rome with the Star of Saint Ermyntrude.

"During the first years of her life in the convent Doña Rosalinda was conspicuous for her piety and strenuous penitence. The sounds of flagellation brought admiring groups of nuns outside the door of her cell. At times she would kneel all night in the chapel repeating Ave Marias on her rosary. During High Mass she would constantly fall into ecstasies and would have to be propped up by *priedieus* that were rigid and stiff as a board. Nuns suffering from various ailments soon evoked her help, believing that the mere touch of her hands was enough to alleviate pain and disease itself.

"Rosalinda, who had extensive knowledge of herbs, installed a small dispensary in the convent where she performed many successful cures. I am now tempted to think that Rosalinda's prayers were more in the nature of incantations, and that she was well versed in witchcraft before she ever entered the convent.

"Rosalinda alone attended the old Abbess on her death bed, and who knows by what black powers she obtained the title of Abbess even before the poor lady had expired.

"After the death of the old Abbess the convent routine underwent many changes invisible to the world outside the walls of the convent. Spiritual supervision of the nuns was in charge of the Bishop of Trève les Frêles. Nobody would have dared criticize anything approved by such a high dignitary of the church.

"In the darkest hours of night the convent chapel became the scene of orgiastic dancing and strange chants in unknown tongues. Weird costumes, pageantry and feasting became the order of the day at the Convent of Santa Barbara.

"Relays of foreign craftsmen came to the convent to redecorate the sumptuous apartments of the Abbess. The octagonal tower became the centre of much activity. The North Wing was chosen by Doña Rosalinda as her own special domain, the octagonal tower forming the main construction of this part of the building. The upper chamber was converted into an observatory, open terraces on all sides affording a complete survey of the Heavens. The reception chamber and sleeping alcove were situated underneath the observatory, which could be reached conveniently by a spiral staircase.

"Scarlet silk studded with little purple and gold Griffins constituted the wall hangings in these chambers. The furniture, made of dark odiferous wood, was carved like all the beasts in creation. Brocade, gorgeously embroidered toreador capes dripped casually from the Abbess's throne, which was carved with her own emblem of Swords and Pomegranates.

"Parquet floors of ebony and white magnolia wood inlaid with silver angels and bronze medallions of the apostles was the sumptuous ground under Doña Rosalinda's small feet. There was something disquieting that such holy beings should be constantly trodden upon by the Abbess. A Persian carpet was occasionally laid for the reception of special visitors.

"A Chinese bookcase decorated with ivory lotus columns and kneeling horses made of the finest jade and as plump as pigs enclosed the personal library of Doña Rosalinda.

"Her books were bound with the hides of various animals, according to their specific contents. Special manuscripts would be bound with ostrich skin or wolf hide. A breviary of a more frivolous nature might be clad with ermine fur or moleskin. A Quabbalistic document by Agrippa von Nettesheim was clad in rhinocerous horn delicately engraved with the horoscope of Queen Hatshepsut. The Liber Spirituum and the Grimorium Verum was covered with Dodo skins studded with small rubies and seed pearls.

"It would be impossible to follow the devious reasons that made the Abbess thus attire her eccentric literature, however that she set the utmost importance to her rare and often wicked books was apparent to anyone who knew her even slightly.

"Indeed she spent most of her days locked in her apartments studying these volumes and writing long commentaries on many a strip of the finest parchment. At nightfall she would mount the spiral staircase to the observatory where she manipulated her forbidden knowledge with I know not what Magic induced by the celestial bodies of the stars.

"The return of the Bishop of Trève les Frêles from the East brought the Abbess temporarily out of retirement. Banquets especially prepared by cooks from abroad were given in honour of the Bishop. Prelates of various ranks were entertained at these feasts.

"The Bishop himself brought gifts for Doña Rosalinda from the East. These included the embalmed head of a white elephant, all sorts of orgiastically embroidered apparel, a huge sandalwood crate full of turkish delight and of course the precious flasks of Musc Madelaine, the ointment said to have been excavated in Nineveh and found beside the mummy of Mary Magdalen herself. This powerful aphrodisiac was no doubt responsible for the supposed miracles attributed to the Abbess after her death.

"A report from Mother Maria Guillerma informed me of the following extravagant occurrence of which she was eyewitness through the ample key hole of Doña Rosalinda's apartments. The keyholes later on became *obscurum per obscurius* after two nuns were

blinded in one eye by a silver needle poked through the opening by the ever perspicacious Abbess.

"They saw Rosalinda and the Bishop inhaling Musc de Madelaine and by some process of *enfleurage* becoming so saturated with the vapours of the ointment that they were surrounded by a pale blue cloud or aura which apparently acted as a volatile element on solid bodies. Thus the Bishop and Abbess were wafted into the air and were suspended, levitating, over the open crate of turkish delight with which they were both gorged. Modesty forbids a full account of the disgusting acrobatics which were then performed in mid air.

"At that period I was too intimidated by the August Dignity of the Bishop to question the matter any further.

"During a certain period after the return of the Bishop, Doña Rosalinda would occasionally give demonstrations for the edification of the rest of the community gathered in the chapel for that purpose. She would turn a luminous blue and levitate over the altar while the nuns swooned with the overpowering vapours of Musc Madelaine which invaded the entire chapel. The orgies which followed these demonstrations are far too horrible to set down with honest ink. Occasionally and much against my will I was obliged to participate myself, through a natural reverence for my superior, the Bishop.

"About the time of the Feast of Corpus Christi the Abbess received a dispatch which threw her into a state of great agitation. This document which is still in my possession reads as follows:

His Royal Highness Prince Theutus Zosimos who has just debarked on Spanish territory sends his most attentive homage to the Lady Abbess, Doña Rosalinda Alvarez Cruz della Cueva of the Convent of Santa Barbara de Tartarus and begs to inform her that he has come to Spain with the determination of reclaiming twenty-one flasks of ointment, Musc Madelaine, which is his rightful property and which he bought for the price of fifteen camels, a hundredweight of wheat grains and six angora goats. The Caravan of his

Highness was savagely attacked near Nineveh by what his Highness mistook for a band of local ruffians. His painful surprise was therefore unlimited when he learnt from a spy sent after the bandits, that the corpulent leader of the Assassins was none other than The Bishop of Trève les Frêles. With some expense and diligence His Highness was informed that the ultimate destination of the said ointment was the Convent of Santa Barbara de Tartarus, Castilla, Spain.

His Royal Highness Prince Theutus Zosimus has no immediate intention of marching belligerently on the convent as he feels assured that the good will and excellent reputation of the Lady Abbess will suffice to return the property of His Highness.

His Highness therefore begs to inform the Abbess, Doña Rosalinda Alvarez Cruz della Cueva, that she may expect a friendly visit from The Prince Himself and Certain Courtiers within a few days and nights, the time, in fact, that it would take to travel from the Mediterranean coast to the hills of Castilla.

Prince Theutus Zosimus will be honoured to be the guest of the Lady Abbess for a few days respite before returning to his own country with all the twenty-one full flasks of the ointment Musc Madelaine, enclosed in sealed earthenware jars.

The Prince offers his most graceful compliments to the Lady Abbess, etc.

"This epistle was sealed with the image of a rampant sea unicorn and the words *Nulla aqua fit quelles, nisi illa que fit de Monoceros aquae nostrae.* These were the arms of the royal house of Theutus Zosimos.

"After a lengthy audience with the Bishop the Abbess summoned her coach and, taking certain provisions for the journey, left the convent the same evening. The secret nature of her mission obliged her to wear the disguise of a bearded nobleman dressed with rich but discreet velvets of midnight violet trimmed with sable and frilled at the throat with lion coloured Irish point lace, very rare in Spain at that time.

"The coach had been especially constructed for secret missions. It never emerged from the convent during daylight so it was little known in the neighbourhood. The interior was fashioned after the usual luxurious tastes of the Abbess, scented sandalwood padded with jewelled antelope skin, cushions and curtains of lemon coloured silk embroidered with Swords and Pomegranates in silver and gold thread, seed pearls, opals and rubies. The exterior of the coach presented a deceptively simple aspect. It was sheathed in silver leaf and bore no ornamentation other than a wreath of mermaids and pineapples around the roof. The coach was drawn by two magnificent Arab mares white as milk and incomparably swift.

"Accompanied by a single trusted servant and the coachman the intrepid Abbess set out on her nocturnal journey towards the south.

"Ninety hours had scarcely passed before Doña Rosalinda intercepted the hired coach carrying the Prince. His Highness was guarded only by two outriders, having left a small army of Moors at Granada to await orders. The outriders were speedily dispatched by Rosalinda's servant, Don Venancio, one of the finest swordsmen in Castilla. In a short space of time the Abbess held the Prince captive in her own coach and the white mares were turned on the road back to Santa Barbara of Tartarus.

"The Prince was so young and comely that the Abbess refrained from doing him any bodily injury; his rich apparel and black skin, small surly beard and flashing eyes impressed her so favourably that she decided to keep him as her constant attendant. The fact that Theutus Zosimos had by no means agreed to this honour did not affect the decision of the Abbess. She sat smiling to herself while the Prince kicked and swore in his own language, caught in the brawny grip of Don Venancio the Swordsman.

"The journey back to Santa Barbara de Tartarus must have been a spectacle of no mean savour. The account of the Abbess, however, was restrained and she refused to be questioned on her return. Deductions of the situation were possible, however, thanks to certain caustic remarks made by the Bishop, and the attitude of

Prince Theutus Zosimus left absolutely no doubt on the general aspect of the situation.

"Reconstructing the journey without details, I picture the Prince becoming slowly aware of the smiling cavalier in the coach. The cavalier, who was of course the Abbess in disguise, aroused the perverted interest of the young man. Certain unnatural oriental customs having already warped his manhood, the Prince made improper advances to Doña Rosalinda who, under the illusion that the Prince recognized her as a lady in disguise, willingly accepted the gallantries of the handsome youth. These advances cannot have gone far, however, for when they arrived at the convent the prince still thought that the Abbess was a gentleman. When she appeared before him smilingly attired in her normal robes he turned coldly aside and gave insinuating glances at the Bishop.

"Moreover once Theutus Zosimus became aware that he was the prisoner of the Abbess, who had also robbed him of the precious flasks of Musc Madelaine, he fell into such a deep trance of melancholia that his life was endangered. Refusing all food and drink he lay prostrate on the dragon couch in the private alcove of the Abbess. After a few days his dusky complexion turned cadmium yellow and his flashing eyes sunk into his head like two stagnant wells.

"The Abbess, whose dominating passion had always been unholy curiosity, decided to give the sick prince a small quantity of Musc Madelaine in a tisane. So far nobody had actually absorbed the powerful ointment by mouth; Doña Rose and the Bishop had always obtained the desired results simply by inhaling the vapours. After certain calculations in the observatory upstairs the Abbess concocted a brew with vervaine leaves, honey, some drops of rose water and a tablespoonful of Musc Madelaine. The Bishop, who already had a certain paternal fondness for the Prince and would no doubt have raised objections to this experiment, happened to be on a short journey to Madrid. Certain ecclesiastic matters concerning the diocese of Santa Barbara de Tartarus were now pressing for attention; the petty nobility whose taxes had been

raised due to the exigencies of luxurious life in the convent had sent complaints to the Archbishop, who had sent a dispatch to the Bishop requiring his presence in Madrid. All this was merely a matter of form as the Archbishop himself had a taste for comfort and in no way expected any reduction of the taxes. The petty nobility were given the impression that all was well, since high dignitaries of the Church were conducting such important conferences on their behalf in the capital.

"Once the Witch Brew (it cannot be named otherwise) was concocted, the Abbess had me summoned to her presence. I was bade open the jaws of the Prince while the Abbess poured the terrible liquid down his gullet. The unfortunate youth was so weak that the whole operation was quite simple, although I cannot say that my own conscience felt entirely easy. Deep in my heart I felt that the Sinful Ointment should never even have entered a Christian Community, nevertheless I would scarcely have dared to disobey the Abbess, whose forceful personality always petrified my will.

"Once Theutus Zosimus had forcefully swallowed the last drop of The Brew he entered a series of convulsions which were frightful to observe. The expression of mild amusement on the face of Doña Rosalinda was further proof of a callous soul.

"No doubt the weak condition and unmanly nature of the Prince prevented the usual manifestations. Instead of shooting through the ceiling as the Abbess had no doubt hoped, the Prince simply lay on the bed flapping his arms feebly and quacking like a duck in the last extremities of its existence. Turning his bloodshot eyes on the Abbess, the unfortunate Prince stated that he had been turned into a female nightingale that was singing for her mate. The confusion of his mind had somehow transformed the Prince into a bird. After what seemed a long period Theutus Zosimus finally gathered strength and arose from the couch. Flapping and quacking he ran up the stairs to the observatory, closely followed by the Abbess and myself. Even if we had so desired I doubt if we would have had time to prevent the unhappy result of the Abbess's

experiment. With staring eyes and foaming lips Prince Theutus Zosimus climbed onto the parapet surrounding the observatory. Then, crying out that he was Queen of the Nightingales, he leapt off to a violent death ninety feet below.

"The rest of that ill-omened night was spent burying the Prince in the kitchen garden.

"After the death of Theutus Zosimus the Bishop of Trève les Frêles seemed to languish. His appetite seemed slightly impaired and he even lost a small quantity of weight. Naturally the Abbess had not informed the Bishop that the Prince was dead. She merely said that during his absence in Madrid she herself had persuaded the Prince to return peacefully to his country. Moreover, she assured the Bishop, the Prince had suddenly imposed certain gallantries upon her person that she had seen fit to satisfy, in exchange for the twenty-one flasks of Musc Madelaine. It is doubtful if the Bishop actually believed the whole story, although he accepted it without commentary and continued to languish.

"Owing, therefore, to an impaired state of health, the Bishop decided to return for a while to Provence, where the bracing air, he said, would rapidly restore his usual exuberance. However I do believe that the news of a new asset to the ecclesiastical music of Avignon stimulated his departure. We were told by a minstrel, who had passed through the city in question, that a bevy of ravishing blonde choirboys had arrived from the British Isles and that their delicate voices could only be compared to an angelic host. The minstrel further informed us that the boys were under the patronage of a small group of Knight Templars who had escaped the purge and had been hiding in Ireland. The persecuted Knight Templars, said the minstrel, had continued to initiate devotees to the order which flourished under the patronage of certain Irish Nobility.

"The Bishop accordingly left for Avignon in the company of a few servants, armed for the hazards of the journey.

"The Abbess once more retired to the privacy of the octagonal tower and pursued her studies. The routine of the convent resumed

a more peaceful atmosphere, and the excited condition of the sisters seemed to abate enough for them to go about their duties clothed and in their right minds.

"As confessor of the Convent I felt my duty obliged me to impose certain penances on the nuns for their orgiastic behaviour during the sojourn of the Bishop. I even suggested to the Abbess herself a slight penance, consisting of three rosaries a week and the present of a few candles to the Blessed Virgin. However she laughed so much when I suggested this that I was obliged to retire pained and somewhat abashed.

"During her life time this woman always managed to impose herself so much on other ordinary mortals that they accepted her superiority without question. No matter how my conscience assured me that she was a manifest profanity to the dogmas of the holy catholic faith I nevertheless found myself weak and supple under her iron will.

"At that period we received visits from different prelates, among which was a cardinal from the Vatican. The convent underwent a rapid revision under the acute observation of the Abbess. She installed herself in an ordinary cell in the West Wing and by the time the cardinal arrived she had put all the statues of the saints right side up and caused the goats' horns to be removed from the top of the Holy Tabernacle. Whenever the cardinal happened to be in the vicinity of her cell the Abbess beat her straw mattress with a whip to give the illusion that she indulged in daily flagellation. She occasionally allowed the cardinal to see her bathed in the pale blue aura of Musc Madelaine, although without the intimate collaboration of a gentleman levitation was not possible. The cardinal, convinced of the saintly nature of the Abbess, returned to Rome with glowing reports of the convent of Santa Barbara de Tartarus. Later these reports must have influenced the Pope favourably towards Rosalinda's canonization.

"*Sunt enim plerique libri adeo obscure scripte, ut a solis auctoribus suis percipiantur.* If this quotation referred to the human soul instead of books I feel it would apply very nicely to the Abbess of Santa Barbara. To this day I doubt very much if it would be possible for

an ordinary human being to penetrate the labyrinth of Doña Rosalinda's heart.

"Summer and winter passed before we received news from the Bishop. It was during the ides of March when the first dispatch arrived from Avignon. Doña Rosalinda had been uncommonly restless since early January and had been taking numerous nocturnal rides in the mountains under her usual disguise, a gentleman of nobility with a short reddish beard. I had sought to discourage these excursions on the grounds that some wandering peasant might one day see her enter the portals of the convent. My admonitions were of no avail however. She would careen into the night mounted on her black stallion, Homunculus. The fiery steed would return to his stable staggering with fatigue and lathered from head to rump after these extravagant rides. Some secret torment seemed to drive the Abbess far into the night, where she tried in vain to quiet her inner turbulence by riding Homunculus unmercifully enough to break his stout heart. Whether she reached this degree of inner agitation because of a lack of progress in her esoteric studies, or whether it was merely due to boredom was impossible for me to know.

"A small incident at that time had caused murmuring amongst the peasants. Some stray dogs had dug up the corpse of Prince Zosimo and had run into the hamlet carrying different portions of his already decomposed body. The morsels of bone and flesh were however still recognisably human and the local magistrate had shown some interest in the original identity of the corpse. It is possible that the Abbess used this embryo scandal as an excuse for her ensuing journey although I think the real reason concerned her own interior unrest and of course the missive from the Bishop which ran as follows:

Gracious Rosalinda, Flos Aeris Aureus, or should I say Esteemed Abbess?

You are no doubt expecting news of my death and burial since so many moons have passed since my departure and I have neither written nor sent verbal messages. My days and even nights have been spent in such continual and strenuous

activity that I must pray you to find pardon in your heart for omitting to send news.

Upon my departure I had not intended such a long sojourn in Avignon. As you know I merely intended to recuperate my health and spirits in the bracing air of Provence and stimulate the soul with angelic music from young throats. My immediate proposition was thereupon a speedy return to Santa Barbara de Tartarus in order to continue to strive towards our mutual goal. The fact that I have remained so long is entirely due to events here which have taken such an extraordinary turn. Our triumph in The Art may indeed depend upon our success here in Avignon.

You will no doubt remember that the minstrel who first brought news from Provence made indirect allusions to The Order of the Knight Templars and actually went so far as to insinuate their presence in this city. Certain Nordic choirboys under their tuition being the veil, so to speak, for a possible Templar Centre in France.

We all know the uncanny power of minstrels to derive news from any place they pass, so the idea that the fellow in question was in possession of such facts will not unduly surprise you. Let me return to the first few weeks of my arrival in Avignon. After an exceptionally tedious journey I spent a few days of retreat in the Palace at Trève les Frêles. These days were passed prostrate in my own downy bed, which was a paradise indeed after the jolting coach. You know how very tender my posterior region becomes after long exposure to a hard seat. Berthe Louise attended my delicate condition with her usual tender care and concocted a marvellous aromatic oil with which she massaged this almost paralyzed region of my body. I was obliged to lie on my face for forty-eight hours before I felt the possibility of reclining on cushions to take refreshment. Game being plentiful this season, I was luckily able to stimulate my failing strength with roast partridges, wild pig cooked in excellent local wine, young venison and stuffed woodcock.

Finally I felt strong enough to negotiate a few leagues, as far as Avignon, in order to refresh my soul with artistic enjoyment in the form of elevated music. As you know, song is the food of the soul, and I was impatient to get to the cathedral to hear the Nordic choirboys sing Mass.

I will not enter into a lengthy ecstatic description of those gentle singers. Let me say simply that if they indeed resemble angels then let me enter paradise and frolic amongst the cherubins. Such delicate fair skins and innocent blue eyes! Their pure trilling song transformed the mass into an experience of pure delight. This, My Dear Rosalinda, is something I feel sure you have never experienced.

After a few superficial difficulties and slight trials such as dining with the Archbishop, I was soon able to get an introduction to the singers, and therefore, I opened my small palace in Avignon, where I took up my abode. On various occasions I entertained the whole choir, who were willing to give short recitals of gothic chant for the edification of the other guests, people of quality from local properties. I was of course obliged to give them some remuneration, and this took a rather heavy toll on the gold I obtained in the East. The expense, however, was not long in bringing its reward, in the form of what I may describe without exaggeration as a celestial friendship. One of the elder boys discovered the usual adolescent impediment in his vocal chords and was thus unable to take part in the choir. I therefore undertook his spiritual instruction and gave him a permanent apartment in the palace.

This boy, I may say, is not only exceptionally beautiful and formed like young Adonis, but is also a gifted poet. The Irish people, I am told, are often favoured with a gift for verse. The boy, Angus, comes from simple stock and is of such a naturally fine nature that one would expect him to have emerged from a Grecian temple rather than the wilds of Ireland. I passed many an evening of fragrant charm in the company of the vivacious youth. We would discuss all

subjects, from Egyptian Magic to Chinese Music, certain frivolities amongst the ancient Greeks, hunting with Irish deerhounds, and the effect of certain herbs. Angus often surprised me with his acute judgment and knowledge of many abstruse subjects. In one of such simple heritage this was as delightful as it was mysterious.

Although I occasionally wondered at the boy's unusual culture I did not pursue the subject too far, for, as you know Rosalinda, happiness is a wraith that never did bear too much meddlesome questioning. I bathed, so to speak, in golden light, unthinking as a soaring bird.

This pleasant state of affairs lasted for about a month, until the arrival of a certain person from England by the name of Sir Hermatrod Siras. This individual must have learnt of the presence of Angus in the palace from his colleagues, the Knight Templars, and his information as to our relationship was unpleasantly accurate. I had forgotten up to the meeting with Sir Hermatrod that the boys were the supposed disciples of the Order. The information of the Minstrel, therefore, was all entirely correct.

Although belonging to the notoriously pig-headed race of Britain, Sir Hermatrod proved himself open to negotiation. I learnt that the Templars were indeed setting up a nucleus of their order in Provence and that they needed sustenance like everybody else.

With the promise of gifts including gold, precious stones and rare perfumes, I was finally able to persuade Sir Hermatrod to leave the Boy Angus under my spiritual tuition, at least for the present.

My tactful persuasion gave fruits, and I learnt a certain amount about the mysterious brotherhood from my protegé. It appeared that since the persecution began a number of Knight Templars had fled under cover, and part of their number had found hospitality in Ireland. An ancient fortress on the west coast had been put at their disposition and was sponsored by the family descendents of King Malcolm, the Moorheads. Now this family, as their name implies, took a

prominent role in the crusades, but had quarrelled with the clergy over the distribution of booty acquired in the East. They were therefore inclined towards friendly relations with the Knight Templars when these fell from the favour of the Church. Secretly the Order flourished and grew in Ireland. Initiates were accepted from noble families, and occasionally from commoners showing a favourable disposition towards the exigencies of the Templars.

For some generations Irish soil proved fruitful for their activities. With time however, the necessity of sowing new centres in other countries became apparent and now, for some fifty years, they had been secretly organizing groups over the continent.

Now, My Dear Flos Acris Aureus, we come to the culmination of my missive. One evening the boy Angus, having partaken of more wine than was prudent for one of such tender years, confided to me the Grand Arcanum of the Order, or rather the living symbol of such. He let me understand that the Knight Templars in Ireland were in possession of the Grail. This wonderful cup, as you know, was said to be the original chalice which held the elixir of life and belonged to the Goddess Venus. She is said to have quaffed the magic liquid when she was impregnated with Cupid, whereupon he leapt in the womb and, absorbing the pneuma, became a God. The story follows that Venus, in her birth pangs, dropped the cup and it came hurtling to earth, where it was buried in a deep cavern, abode of Epona the Horse Goddess.

For some thousands of years the cup was safely in the keeping of the subterranean Goddess, who was known to be bearded and a hermaphrodite. Her name was Barbarus.

It is possible that you have heard the legend before. I must say I found the name most striking, through obvious associations.

The Goddess Barbara was worshipped as the life giver or womb, and her priests were generally supposed to be chosen hermaphrodites.

Seth, the son of Noah, was supposed to be the first to march upon the sanctuary of this Goddess. The priests were murdered and the Grail was stolen, the sanctuary desecrated; according to the legend the Grail lay in the hands of the tribe of Seth and was stolen in turn by the Knight Templars during the crusade.

Later stories sprang up around the Grail, and its magic was erroneously attributed to Christian sources.

Whatever the truth may be concerning the great antiquity of the grail its wonderful power is beyond any doubt, and certain precise indications make me believe that what Angus told is true.

Chère Mutus Rosarium, you will at once appreciate the necessity to at least see the wonderful cup and if possible to restore it to the Goddess Barbarus, or should I give her a more recent title? Who knows that this might be a means of eventually returning stolen property to the original owner, Venus?

I advise you to place a deputy abbess at the head of the convent and set out soon for Avignon. I can promise you a comfortable suite in the palace and a cuisine which will, at least, rival that of the convent. We may be obliged afterwards to travel to the Knight Templars' fortress in Ireland, so bring ample provision for the journey. Although the Grail may already be in France, I doubt if it would be moved before they are living under settled conditions.

Take care to provide yourself with plenty of cushions for the journey, unless you want to sleep on your face for a week after you arrive. The roads are truly execrable.

Ever your Tender Admirer and Soul Brother in all that mutually binds us together.

<div style="text-align:right">Fernand, Bishop of Trève les Frêles.</div>

"Before her departure the Abbess hid the flasks of Musc Madelaine. Although I searched the whole convent later on I never

could find the remaining flasks of ointment. Now I know that she must have hidden them in the crypt under the church where she was eventually buried. At that time it did not occur to me that the tombs of past abbesses of the convent could be the hiding place. Also a certain terror of the sinister vault kept me, no doubt, from considering that place as a possibility.

"So after careful preparation the Abbess donned her disguise and left in the silver coach drawn by the two white mares. An outrider, mounted on Homunculus the black stallion, accompanied the coach.

"Sister Teresa de Gastélum Xavier was appointed deputy Abbess. This nun was the personal attendant of Doña Rosalinda, and entirely devoted to the eccentric Abbess.

"Teresa de Gastélum Xavier probably came from Moorish stock and had a dark complexion and morose secretive ways; she installed herself in the octagonal tower and it was extremely difficult to gain access into the Abbess's apartments without her knowledge.

"With a certain amount of diligence I did succeed on various occasions to get in and look through Doña Rosalinda's personal effects, and in this manner came to be in possession of certain written documents and letters which helped to give insight into the character of the Abbess. As the convent confessor I considered it my duty to keep informed as far as possible of the happenings concerning Santa Barbara de Tartarus. Doña Rosalinda was naturally the main focal point of my interest. Vulgar curiosity in no way stimulated me; I was merely performing my duty as the Spiritual Director of the Community.

"Mystery surrounds the journey of the Abbess, who was absent for almost two years. She must have spent more than half this time in the West of Ireland near the fortress of the Knight Templars, if not within the stronghold itself. Knowing the diabolically astute nature of Doña Rosalinda I am inclined to believe that she did indeed manage to spend a considerable time inside the fortress, although how this difficult feat was performed it is impossible to say. Probably no one but the Bishop of Trève les Frêles suspected

that the bearded cavalier was really the Abbess, at least not for some time; and whoever did eventually discover her female identity kept the secret, otherwise Doña Rosalinda would never have left Ireland alive.

"The condition of the Abbess when she did finally return to Santa Barbara de Tartarus left no doubt whatever that one person at least knew her to be a woman. I say a 'Person,' although considering the incredible events around the death of the Abbess I sometimes recoil with a nameless doubt.

"After the Abbess was dead I did happen to come into possession of a scroll which was written in Hebrew and which I was finally able to translate with the help of a Jew who traded spices in Madrid.

"This scroll was accompanied by another document in Latin which evidently referred to the sojourn of Doña Rosalinda in Ireland and most likely to her stay in the fortress of the Knight Templars. Here I give both documents, the first being the translation from the Hebrew.

He [the Sinner] shall not be absolved by expiations nor by the lustral waters of sea and river. He called Set of the tribe out of Egypt shall be called Unclean throughout the ages until the Cup of Pneuma shall return unto the Daughters calledAriouth of Tartarean;

That all His [Set] iniquities shall be atoned for by the submission of his soul to the [female] Foreign Stranger [otherwise translated as Bar-bar-a] Who shall once more replenish the Cup with Holy Pneuma by [a] ritual joining to the yellow [or golden] Horned God, Keeper of the Most Holy Vessel.

At the beginning the two spirits which are known as Twins are the one Female and the Other Male. They established at the beginning Life, the Pneuma and the Holy Cup to hold the Pneuma.

And when these two Spirits Met such was the manner of the birth of the Winged One [or the Feathered Hermaphrodite, Sephirá].

For since the Cup has not rendered fruit. The sterile jailors of the cup having banished Her from Her Most Rightful Realm in the Caverns of Her Most Secret Mysteries

Epona, Barbarus, Hekate.

And the children of the Planet will forget and not find the path of the Years and will forget the new moons and the seasons and they

will go wrong as to all the order of time and of the running bodies in the Heavens. They will thus perpetrate abominations, for the cup lies empty and sterile under the rule of Set who is Yehowá The Revenger.

And when the three moons rise together and obscure the light of the sun there will be lamentations and gnashing of bones for they have forgotten their origin and no longer know the roots of the Tree.

Behold the Wise One is robber of Her Holy Vessel which lies in bondage of the Sterile Brothers, which lies empty and forsaken of the most miraculous Pneuma.

Woe unto the children of earth who worship a trinity of men. Woe unto the Sterile Brothers who have torn the cup from Her keeping.

This ambiguous document was unsealed, but the quality of the papyrus must have been of ancient date. The second scroll was also unsigned and written by some unknown hand:

Et volabo cum ea in coelo et dicam tunc. Vivo ego in aeternum. Foreign Strangers have entered the Rath of Conor [evidently the name of the fortress where the Knight Templars were gathered since the persecution]. A Spanish noble accompanied by a corpulent French Bishop from Provence. They have come to solicit initiation into the Order of the Knight Templars.

The Grand Master is making a preliminary examination of the travellers.

Satisfaction has been granted to the Spanish noble, Don Rosalendo de Tartaro. He is to begin instruction under Sir Aillen. The case of the Bishop is being withheld for further inspection.

The Rath of Conor has been shaken by an earthquake and the community is just regaining an orderly routine which was thrown into chaos from the shock. A subterranean murmur is still audible from the bowels of the earth.

The rumors from underground still prevail and are said to issue from the vault where we keep the Arcanum.

The Grand Master has called a General Assembly in the Octagonal Chamber, we believe the subterranean murmur is

connected with the Arcanum. The Grand Master will no doubt illuminate us further on the alarming occurrence.

A wandering bard seeking shelter has just arrived at the Rath of Conor, he calls himself Taliessin.

The Grand Master has informed us that the vault of the Arcanum is to be opened after being sealed for the last two hundred years. This momentous decision was taken last night after a conference lasting for five hours.

The Bard Taliessin has kept us amused with humourous songs of the earthquake. He has improvised a ballad telling that the Arcanum has stirred in its sleep because of the arrival of a lady. This made us all laugh merrily. No woman has entered the Rath of Conor since it was donated to the Order by the Moorheads.

Tonight we are to draw lots in order that fate shall decide who shall enter the dreaded vault alone and unaccompanied according to the tradition.

Sir Sean of Liath is to be the first Knight Templar to enter the vault of the Arcanum since it was sealed by Sir Rufus two hundred years ago after the mysterious death of twelve Knights of The Order.

Sir Sean of Liath will meditate all night by the Altar of The Spear before his ordeal.

He will be purified with water from the well of Annwn and wear the silver sword won by the Knight Templars from the conquered people of the Sidhe.

Terrible happenings have plunged the Rath of Conor into deep mourning. Four of the most honoured Knights of the Order have been blasted to the death.

After the vault was ritually unsealed by the Grand Master each successive knight to enter the chamber of the Arcanum has met a frightful and inexplicable death.

Each one has issued from the dread chamber convulsed and raving of a frightful horned apparition that glitters as of burnished gold. Then with blood pouring from their eyes and mouth they expire cursing the Grail.

May God Have Mercy on Their Souls.

Sir Sean of Liath, Sir Thomas Vervin, Sir Stanislaus Brath, Sir Wilfred Donnegan. All have met untimely and fearful ends. They will be buried with All the honours of the Order in the East Crypt.

Taliessin sings that only a lady may enter the presence of the Horned God and come to no harm. An unknown stranger from the nether world is to come and replenish the cup. All this sounds like talk of the Sidhe with whom Taliessin may be secretly allied.

To our general consternation Don Rosalendo de Tartaro has volunteered to enter the vault of the Arcanum. This would be excessively unorthodox as he is not yet ordained.

However since this brave cavalier will be unlikely to survive the adventure general opinion is in favour of allowing him a glorious death and ordination on the deathbed.

Taliessin sings a curious roundelay which sounds like advice for Don Rosalendo.

It is increasingly probable that the Bard had dealings with the Sidhe although this would be impossible to prove.

The refrain of his roundelay bids the Spanish cavalier carry 'Something to strike and cut and bind.' He then refers to something feathered 'to be born,' which may mean some kind of bird.

Don Rosalendo has entered the twelve hour meditation in his own apartments. He has solicited the use of the silver sword of the Sidhe, a willow branch and a length of rope. He will carry a small flacon of a substance he refuses to name and which is of his personal property. He carries seven flacons of this substance in an ebony casket engraved with luminous unicorns.

We are anticipating the Death of the brave Spaniard with heavy hearts, *'et invenitur in omni loco et in quolibet tempore et apud omnem rem, cum inquisitio aggravat inquirentem.'*

The Spaniard has emerged Alive from the dreaded Vault. The triumph of a layman over Ordained Knight Templars is causing much discussion.

Six Knights and the Grand Master witnessed the entry of Don Rosalendo Tartaro into the Arcanum chamber where he passed three whole hours behind closed doors.

Finally he emerged, smiling, unscathed and emitting a pale blue light. He still bore the Sidhe sword and the willow branch, but the flacon and cord had been left behind in the chamber.

According to traditional ritual he was searched at sword's point and to our unbounded horror we found he carried the Grail itself concealed under his cloak. Four of the knights fell prostrate on their faces while one fled. The Grail emitted a luminous essence

impossible to behold. The sixth Knight, Sir Pheneton, held his ground and obliged Don Rosalendo to return the cup to the vault under pain of death should he refuse.

After much deliberation the Grand Master has decided to spare the life of Don Rosalendo for his Gallantry. However for Sacriligeous Dishonesty Don Rosalendo has been requested to leave the Rath of Conor immediately together with the Bishop and all their luggage, never to return, under pain of execution.

The Bard Taliessin will accompany them at his own request.

Sir Pheneton Sanderson has been awarded the Iron Pentagon for his valiant conduct. The subterranean murmur has entirely ceased and all is as still as death in the vault.

"These documents concerning the sojourn of the Abbess abroad are so incomplete that many mysteries are unexplained. Since I found the two scrolls amongst her personal effects after her death I suppose she must have stolen them from the fortress of Rath of Conor. How this was achieved only Doña Rosalinda could know.

"As I already said, two years passed before the Abbess returned to Spain. A courier preceeded her arrival by some seven days, bearing a message that all should be prepared for her imminent arrival at Santa Barbara de Tartarus. Some apprehension and a great deal of excitement prevailed throughout the community.

"When she finally arrived however few of the nuns witnessed her entry into the convent, for the hour was before dawn, the zero hour, as they say. My own apartment happening to be situated over the main Zaguan, I was awoken by the sound of horse and coach. Dressing hurriedly, I descended to welcome Doña Rosalinda back to the convent.

"Although the Abbess was swathed in a long dark cloak it was impossible to mistake the fact that she carried an enormous belly, at least twice the size of an ordinary pregnancy and in the ninth month before delivery.

"When the servants had transported all Doña Rosalinda's effects into the octagonal tower she herself retired inside, walking slowly and laboriously. Mother Gastélum de Xavier attended her during the last three days of her life.

"The third day I was summoned to the tower by Sister Fabiolina, who had taken the responsibility upon her own shoulders to call me, having fallen into a state of collapse on having witnessed the terrible events in the tower.

"The Abbess was lying in her death agony, the hour was midnight. I still shake with ague when the terrible sight returns before my mind's eye. For Doña Rosalinda, who had always been a thin woman, had swollen to such a monstrous size as to resemble a small whale, and she had turned coal black. The swelling process had attained its utmost dimension and she slowly floated into the air, where she remained suspended for a moment. Then a sudden quaking came over the body, followed by a report louder than any known cannon and an explosion of such violence that I was thrown against the wall. All that remained of the Abbess of Santa Barbara de Tartarus was a morsel of damp black skin no larger than a pocket handkerchief, and this lay on the bed.

"Pungent fumes so heavy as to resemble a thundercloud, and with a most dreadful stench filled the death chamber. Reeling from the shock of this most awesome spectacle, I did not at once become aware of a small object or luminous body, suspended and flapping in the density of the fumes. A short period passed before I recognized a boy, no bigger than a barn owl, luminously white and winged, that fluttered near the ceiling. He bore a bow and arrows, but the penetrating light that issued from his body prevented me from a more detailed examination. The stench of the gasses released from the dead Abbess had now turned into a heavy and most exquisite perfume, like Musc and jasmine.

At this moment the terrified sisters, having heard the frightful explosion of Doña Rosalinda, rushed into the Tower, accompanied by Monseñor Rodriguez Zepeda, a priest from Madrid. All that they witnessed was the perfume, or Odour of Sanctity as they called it, and a momentary vision of the winged boy who disappeared up the spiral staircase into the observatory and was no more to be seen. Of course they took him to be an angel.

"The awkward fact that the Abbess left only a morsel of dark skin as the remains of her mortal body did not deter the sisters from

proclaiming her a saint. On the contrary, they held that she had ascended to Heaven like the Blessed Virgin, leaving only an angel and the Odour of Sanctity behind. The scrap of skin was laid out amongst roses and lilies and afterwards interred in a magnificent coffin big enough to hold three Abbesses. The burial was performed in the convent crypt which I believe I already mentioned.

"Monseñor Rodriguez Zepeda and fifty nuns had all witnessed the scene after the explosion of the Abbess, therefore any testimony I might have volunteered would never have turned their conviction that the miracles were indeed from Heaven and not from the depths of Hell, as I know beyond doubt.

"This document was written by Dominico Eucaristo Deseos, ancient confessor of the Convent of Santa Barbara de Tartarus, burned at the stake at the age of ninety-seven by Order of the Pope (Name illegible.)

> *In te inimicos nostros ventilabimus cornu. Et in nomine tuo spernemus insurgentes in nobis. Cornu veru nostrum Christus est, idem et nomen Patris in quo adversaris nostri vel ventilantur vel spernuntur.*

A footnote written in cramped writing and faded ink bore the following words:

> Putrefactio without which triumph of the opus cannot be attained.
> Cup and Pneuma for release of SS.
> 'And it hath changed my darkness into light, and it hath rent the chaos which surrounded me."

<p style="text-align:center">* * *</p>

Here ends the tractate of Doña Rosalinda.

By hanging a blanket over the window I was able to read the entire script without betraying the fact that the light was on well into the small hours of the morning.

So this was the history of the winking Abbess. I must say I was

not disappointed, although I found her final disintegration somewhat depressing. During the narrative I had become affectionately attached to the intrepid and energetic Abbess. The fact that the snooping priest, Dominico Eucaristo Deseos, had done his best to portray her in a pernicious light, hardly distorted the purity of her original image. She must have been a most remarkable woman.

I longed to question Christabel Burns further. How, for instance, had the portrait of the Abbess come to America, and why was it hanging here in the Institution? I meant to question Christabel after sunrise, as soon as I could find her. Events turned out in such a manner however that I was unable to talk to Christabel for some days; indeed during this period few of us would have considered any other subject of discussion than the dramtic circumstances which I am now to relate.

Owing to my perusal of the history of the Abbess I overslept and was woken by Anna Wertz. She was talking and gesticulating as she shook me awake. An excited state being the usual condition of Anna Wertz, I did not take any particular notice until she handed me my hearing trumpet and forced it, so to speak, into position.

"I had just dropped in to ask her advice about a piece of embroidery I intended to apply on some velvet I happened to have for some time, a fine piece of velvet in its way, and really looked like new although I must have had it before I came here. As you know I never get a moment of time to myself to take the smallest recreation and I do enjoy just sitting alone and sewing beads into some fanciful sort of flower, but people cannot be expected to understand one gets more pleasure from being alone and working at something inspired than just running off one's feet at all sorts of tasks which really are the responsibility of other people."

Banging the table with my hearing trumpet, I shouted: "For the love of peace Anna come to the point, what ails you?" Experience had taught me that any kind of diffidence in dealing with Anna's monologues was doomed beforehand.

"Well you really don't have to shout, I was just about to explain how she came running out like an escaped steam roller and grabbed me, jibbering, literally jibbering and before I had time to resist, you know how strong she is, she pulled me inside the bungalow and of course the poor thing was stiff and dead, I was so extremely shocked...."

"Anna," I yelled, now thoroughly frightened, "WHAT ARE YOU TALKING ABOUT?"

"Why about Poor Maude, can't you understand, she died during the night, and we are all so upset and as I knew you were friendly with her there I was banging away on your door but nothing seemed to wake you up. Then poor Natacha, you know how very sensitive she is? Well she has had to retire to bed she is so terribly shocked and sad that Doctor Gambit has had to give her sleeping tablets, at least three, although I never did notice that she was such a great friend of Poor Maude, did you?"

No indeed I had not, but I did see the chocolate fudge like an apparition. Chocolate fudge containing something out of a packet that had been meant for somebody else. Poor Maude with her dainty flowered blouses and *Ame de rose* face powder. Her peach crèpe-de-chine cami-knickers which we all envied and which had taken her six months to sew. Timid, sensitive Maude, the only one of our number that had in any way resembled the Dear Old Lady of Tradition, with fluffy white hair, pink cheeks and white teeth. False of course, but white.

It was easy to picture poor Maude sitting under a bower of rambling roses in some old world garden full of hollyhocks and lavender, sewing dainty cami-knickers through all eternity.

I was deeply shocked by the terrible news. Especially as I might have saved her life if only I had warned her when I saw her emerging out of Natacha's igloo, and gone to seek medical attention immediately.

This put me in a dreadfully awkward situation. Should I repeat what I had seen in the kitchen between Natacha and Mrs. Van Tocht? Obviously it seemed best to inform Dr. Gambit immediately, especially as Natacha and Mrs. Van Tocht might

continue making chocolate fudge, having failed to extinguish their victim at the first attempt. This, of course, would make Dr. Gambit wonder why I had been peeking through the window myself, and there was no dignified explanation that I could think of. Common greed or inquisitive nosiness were the obvious conclusions. Perhaps Mrs. Van Tocht and Natacha would go to gaol. I knew of no age limit for imprisonment, especially if it concerned murder; it would still be murder, I supposed, even if they got the wrong victim. In England they would no doubt have undergone capital punishment, in which case I would have to risk saying nothing at all, as nobody could convince me of the morality in deliberately sending somebody to their death.

The whole affair was most disturbing. Poor Maude, I might have saved her.

In the mean time I was fully dressed, but felt no real appetite for breakfast. Anna Wertz was telling me something: "We could easily climb on the roof and look through the skylight, there is a small ladder at the back of the bungalow which is used when the gutters have to be cleaned out. They never seem to clean them out but the ladder is still there. I would like to get a look at poor Maude because we will never see her again. Such a fragile little woman."

Anna was suggesting that we should climb on the roof and spy on Maude's corpse. Horrible and dishonest, from anybody else's point of view, but who would ever expect two old ladies to be perched on a roof?

We had to push our way through a lot of undergrowth in order to be able to approach the bungalow without being seen. I felt as if we were playing at boy scouts. The ladder at the back of the bungalow seemed alarmingly old and the wood looked rotten. Anna Wertz, who had stopped talking for the first time since I had known her, had begun climbing cautiously up the ladder. I hoped she would not find it imperative to give a running commentary once we were up there, as discovery would be ignominious. I hauled myself up the creaking ladder in the wake of Anna Wertz. The roof of the bungalow was flat and had two skylights which emitted light to the rooms below. We installed ourselves over the

one that gave a perfect view of Maude's room. Death had converted Maude's face into a narrow, unrecognizable mask that somehow reminded me of a thin slice of unripe pumpkin. Her mouth was half open, and she stared up at us with an expression of mingled reproach and surprise. Her false teeth stood in a glass of water beside the bed. This accounted, I suppose, for the narrowness of her face. Still fluffy, her white hair frizzed over her dead face.

Mrs. Van Tocht sat at a short distance from the bed. Her face, a foreshortened mass of flesh, betrayed no expression, but her hands seemed to be tearing at each other in ceaseless agitation.

An unknown woman wearing a grey overall came in carrying a towel, a soap dish containing a piece of yellow kitchen soap, and a bucket of water. Her movements were precise and detached. In a methodical way she removed the bedclothes, revealing the entire corpse, which was almost fully dressed. The effects of the poisoned fudge must have started before she had time to put on her nightdress, poor thing. Later I learnt that she had not gone in to supper, informing Mrs. Van Tocht that she felt livery and had a bad migraine. She must have died while everybody was at supper. This would explain why nobody had heard her call in the last moments of agony.

Now the woman in the grey overall was stripping off Maude's clothes. She did this with certain difficulty, as rigor mortis must have set in during the night.

A moment later Anna Wertz was clutching my arm convulsively, and we both almost fell through the skylight onto the incredible sight below. Maude's stark naked corpse was that of a venerable old gentleman.

I shall never quite remember how Anna and I got down the ladder without breaking our necks. We must have negotiated it somehow. We saw Dr. Gambit in the distance, hurrying towards the double bungalow, and hastened to put as much distance as possible between the death chamber and ourselves. As we emerged from the undergrowth we collided with Georgina Sykes, who claimed to have thought she heard a water buffalo under the

bushes and had stopped to make sure. Anna Wertz disappeared as if she had a werewolf after her.

"And what the Hell may I ask were you doing trampling around in the bushes with Anna Wertz?" asked Georgina as I picked twigs out of my hair. "You sounded like a stampede of African water buffalos."

"For goodness sake don't shout so loud," I said anxiously. "Somebody might hear you. Come to the bee pond and I will tell you everything."

"Poor old Maude died of acute cirrhosis of the liver during the night," said Georgina. "The Gambit assembled us in the work room and told us all about how we should use death for renewed Self Conscious Observation. She was no chicken, but one never thinks it happens quite so suddenly."

I decided to tell Georgina the whole unpleasant affair, as I had begun to suspect her life might be in danger. I began tentatively: "Maude could not have died of a liver complaint, her complexion was far too fresh. People who die of cirrhosis have yellow skins like Natacha."

"Maude always plastered her face with pink goo," said Georgina. "You couldn't have told if she was turquoise blue under all that stuff."

"Maude Somers did not die of cirrhosis of the liver." We had arrived at the bee pond, which was deserted by all but the working bees. We sat on a stone bench and I told Georgina the whole story of how I had watched Mrs. Van Tocht and Natacha put poison in the fudge, how Maude had followed Natacha, and afterwards stolen the fatal sweetmeat. Then the dramatic episode on the bungalow roof where we had discovered that dainty, feminine Maude was really a man.

"Suffering cobras!" said Georgina who had gone pale. "The fudge must have been meant for me. She had it all arranged."

The little reconciliation feast that Natacha had offered Georgina near the kitchen had been a deliberately planned murder.

"We had better tell Gambit at once," said Georgina. "They

106

must call in the police. If we were in the United States they would both go to the lethal chamber and be frizzled to lard in the electric chair. I wouldn't mind paying anything up to ten dollars to watch."

"There is no capital punishment here," I told Georgina. "But they might make them work on a chain gang, cracking rocks with pick axes and whipped by colossal nubians wearing red loin cloths."

Georgina made a wry grimace, "All that will happen is that they will be given a nice sitting room in the ladies' jail and they will give fudge parties twice a week and spiritualist séances on Sundays."

"Of course if they prove poor Maude was murdered," I said after some reflection, "Natacha would pretend that she had made the fudge to poison the rats she talked about."

"Whoever heard of making chocolate fudge for rats?" replied Georgina. "They use old lumps of putrified cheese."

We set out to look for Dr. Gambit but only succeeded in finding Mrs. Gambit, who was stirring potato soup in the kitchen.

"Dr. Gambit will not receive anybody today. I think it is very frivolous of you both to ask for an interview about personal problems when the Doctor is worried out of his mind," said Mrs. Gambit with her tightlipped smile.

"This is urgent," said Georgina. "We must see him at once."

"Nevertheless, Dr. Gambit cannot attend to personal matters today," replied Mrs. Gambit. "I will now ask you to attend the cleaning of your own bungalows and go through the day in a controlled and orderly manner, in spite of the sad event which has upset our usual routine."

Obviously it was hopeless to insist further, and we were unable to talk to Dr. Gambit until the following day, after Maude's funeral. This seemed a pity, as they would no doubt have all the trouble of digging her up again, but there was no more we could do.

In the meantime we walked around the garden discussing the whole affair from every possible angle.

"Who would ever have dreamed Maude was really a man in disguise?" I asked Georgina. "All those cami-knickers and dainty blouses. Aren't you surprised out of your life?"

"I am not surprised at all," said Georgina. "I knew Maude was really a man the moment she arrived."

"How could you conceivably have known that?" I asked in astonishment. "She looked more like a woman than any of us."

"I knew Arthur Somers when he had a curio shop in New York," said Georgina. "But there was no reason on earth why I should give away his little secret, seeing that he never did me any harm in his life. Why he should have chosen such an awful name as Maude was his own business."

"But why should he shut himself up in an old ladies' home?" I asked. "Surely he could have found something more amusing. He had a little money of his own, I believe."

"Well, since you know the kernel of the story I might as well tell you the whole thing. It won't do poor Arthur any harm now.

"Years ago, Arthur Somers bought a very small shop on Eighth Avenue which he filled with all sorts of repulsive garbage that he called curios; I used to live next door, with the Abyssinian I told you about. So I used to pop in now and again and chat with Arthur about my little troubles, and we became quite friendly. After a while I learnt that our Arty's antiques were just a front for a small underground business. He sold tiny pink or blue pin-cushions covered with lace and stuffed with marijuana.

"It took me a long time to find out why his clients, who were often brawny deck hands, went in for so many dainty needlework accessories. Arthur made the pin cushions himself. That was how he came to be so handy with a needle. He had a very cosy little business. Lots of people enjoy smoking marijuana, it cheers them up.

"One fine day he rented one of the three rooms over the shop to a lady landscape painter called Veronica Adams, yes, the same Veronica Adams that now inhabits the cement boot near the toadstool where the Marquise lives. She still goes on painting all

those yards of toilet paper. Well, at that period she was a fine figure of a woman and Arthur fell madly in love with her. He didn't even collect the rent. The romantic attachment must have made Arthur careless, because he started selling pink pin-cushions to the New York police by mistake. Things began to get very difficult and Arthur would no doubt have gone to Sing Sing or somewhere like it if he had not been tipped off in time by Nut-Eyed Johnson, who ran a speakeasy in Greenwich Village. So Arthur and Veronica skipped over the border and ran a night club in Laredo. Veronica painted her landscapes whenever she had any free time. She also went in for Saturday Night Strip Tease when there were enough clients. I never actually saw her myself, but it is quite a thought if you look at her now. She must have worn ostrich feathers and beads. I believe Arthur confected the costumes.

"So, there they were, as long as Veronica's figure was able to attract clients. Later on they were able to retire, and after spending some years in the Argentine they came here. Arthur thought a home for senile ladies was a tasteful end to a rather active life. Poor Arthur never bargained at having to share a bungalow with Mrs. Van Tocht. That was a sad blow, but he got used to it eventually. He always made a great point of the virtues of modesty so Mrs. Van Tocht, nosey as she is, never found out the secret. Up till now anyway. That is a schematic history of the life of Arthur Somers, who never expected to get murdered in a home for old ladies, although he might very well have been murdered almost anywhere else."

Georgina seemed saddened as she thought backwards, and I made an effort to change the subject. "I wonder what marijuana tastes like?" I asked, but Georgina had not heard. Perhaps she was thinking about Arthur and Veronica Adams. Maybe she was thinking about the Abyssinian.

Arthur or Maude's funeral was a rather hurried affair. No relations came, so it was only attended by Dr. and Mrs. Gambit. Nobody found out what they thought about Arthur or Maude being a man. They never mentioned this in front of the

community. Veronica went on painting on the toilet rolls. She was so bent one could not see her face or guess if she suffered from the loss of her old lover.

Personally I spent a very bad night, worrying alternately about what I should tell Dr. Gambit and quaking with apprehension when I thought about the sinister plot of Natacha and Mrs. Van Tocht. One would not have expected these kinds of problems in a home for senile old ladies.

Dr. Gambit received Georgina and me shortly before lunch time. His plump face looked unusually grey and he twitched nervously.

"Really," he told us irritably. "Any kind of general advice on the Work can be got from Mrs. Gambit. I am excessively occupied. Please come to the point immediately."

"Easy," said Georgina with her usual courage. "Maude Somers was murdered, she never had cirrhosis of the liver."

Dr. Gambit gave something like a hoarse squeak then, recovering himself, said: "Georgina, you must work strenuously to overcome your diseased imagination."

"Diseased imagination be damned!" said Georgina. "Just listen to Mrs. Leatherby's story about what she saw through the kitchen window."

So I told my story.

"Now," said Dr. Gambit, "if you have quite finished. I may say that I have never heard such a scurrilous piece of defamation in my entire life. I am shocked above all at Georgina, who has been in the Work now for some years. You are both prey to diseased imagination, one of the most deeprooted vices of the human creature. I will organize some private exercises for you both, in order that you may overcome this terrible psychological sickness."

"You must be mad," said Georgina angrily. "You sit there squeaking about psychology while we all might be poisoned at any meal. Van Tocht and Natacha ought to be put in the electric chair."

"That," said Dr. Gambit rising from his chair, "will be quite

sufficient Mrs. Sykes. I will see that you are given a sedative."

"What about the rat poison that Mrs. Gambit bought for Natacha?" I asked. "Surely you will at least ask her to account for that."

"Mrs. Gonzalez," said Dr. Gambit with dignity, "is a most remarkable woman, with a very high degree of extrasensory powers. It would be impossible for either you or Georgina Sykes to understand the delicate mechanism of her mind. This abusive gossip which you have invented only shows that you are fermenting with Envy.

"And now I will bid you good day. Mrs. Gambit will give you a sedative." He opened the door and pushed us out of the study.

Georgina and I had imagined all kinds of reactions, but we were entirely unprepared for a wall of total disbelief. We had nothing at all to say for almost five minutes. The idea of approaching Mrs. Gambit with our account of the murder seemed hopeless.

All during lunch I kept giving Mrs. Van Tocht and Natacha surreptitious glances; Georgina and I ate practically nothing. It did not seem safe.

In the afternoon I was told that I had a visitor and I hurried into the parlour reserved for weekday callers. My surprise and delight were unbounded when I saw Carmella, looking very modish in a long tweed dress.

Carmella's telepathy had told her that something was amiss. She had dreamt about me doing a Viennese waltz with an officer.

"Dancing in dreams means either occult power or trouble," she told me. "So I knew you must be in some sort of trouble."

I took Carmella to my favourite place, the bee pond, and there I poured out the whole story of how poor Maude-Arthur had been murdered by mistake, and how we feared that mistake might be rectified at almost any moment.

"I will give a solution in a few moments," said Carmella, who was rummaging in a large covered basket that she had brought. "In the meantime I had better give you the chocolate biscuits and the

secluded spot in the garden. The bee pond would be well hidden from the house and from observation of the murderesses.

"This is of course a kind of mutiny, and if you are discovered by the authorities they might turn machine guns on you. An armoured car would be most adequate, or even a small tank, although there might be some difficulties in getting these. You would be obliged to ask the collaboration of the army. I am not sure if they lend out tanks, although they might have an old one. In any case the meeting should take place with the greatest secrecy. If you can get people to come hooded it would be better, because then they would not be recognized unless captured and tortured."

Carmella went through this advice several times, then took her leave with a few final instructions, such as putting snipers in the trees around the bee pond, installing secret radio stations and a series of outposts with tom-toms which would relay coded messages.

After Carmella's stimulating visit I was feeling quite excited and happy. It was not long before I met Georgina, to whom I immediately communicated our plans, omitting some of the less practical ones such as the tanks, the snake oil, the secret radio stations and the snipers. I emphasized the hunger strike as not only desirable, but urgently necessary.

"I couldn't have thought of a better idea myself," said Georgina. "We must make the meeting tonight. After dinner everybody can pretend to go to their bungalows as usual, and when the Gambits, Van Tocht and Natacha are nicely tucked in we sally forth and meet at the pond."

"We had better inform Veronica Adams, the Marquise, Christabel and Anna Wertz so they know more or less why we are meeting, and don't let on to Natacha and Mrs. Van Tocht," I said. "People can say they have a stomach ache and can't eat supper. This might even be a good way to initiate the hunger strike."

So, being agreed, we set out to tell the other ladies of our plans.

Dinner that night was a most lugubrious affair. The only

persons to take food were Dr. Gambit, Mrs. Van Tocht and Natacha. Mrs. Gambit had retired early with aspirin and a sick headache. The rest of us sat and watched them eat. The tension was appalling.

"I am not going to attempt to find out why you have all lost your appetites," said Doctor Gambit at the end of the meal, "I will however say this. Hysterical complaints have no place in the Work. Psychosomatic illness kills just as effectively as any other physical disease. If you deliberately allow your lower centres to take hold of your organism you will soon become victims to a mass deteriorisation which may have serious consequences."

With that he dabbed his mouth with a table napkin and rolled it up into the bone napkin ring which we all used. Clean table napkins every day would have made the laundry bill excessive, according to Mrs. Gambit.

Evening recreation in the lounge did not last as late as usual. Everybody was relieved when Dr. Gambit rang the bell and we all retired to our respective habitations.

The Abbess looked down upon us with her sardonic smile.

There was no moon that night, but luckily we all had candles, which were put in each bungalow for occasions when the electricity failed, which it most often did.

By the time we were all assembled at the bee pond it must have been about eleven-thirty. The circumstances were so unusual that I hardly noticed the curious fact that some bees were still buzzing over the still dark water of the fountain. I heard them in some dormant part of my consciousness, although I have since wondered if it were not some acoustic peculiarity produced by my hearing trumpet.

I opened the meeting with a complete enumeration of the facts, which were all substantiated by Georgina. Then biscuits were passed around and there was a general discussion.

We all agreed that a hunger strike was by far the most practical solution, although there was a certain doubt as to how long my supply of chocolate biscuits would keep us alive.

In order to combat the chilly evening air I had brought the hot

water bottle filled with sweet port, and we passed this around now and again. It would really have been a very pleasant gathering if we had not been menaced by starvation at a future date.

"I also have a supply of sweet biscuits that I would be pleased to put at the disposal of the community," said Christabel Burns. "I brought a biscuit for each person in my pockets, as I had also visualised our hungry condition after retiring without dinner. The supply was somewhat limited so I only brought each person one biscuit. Happily Mrs. Leatherby also has a private supply of chocolate biscuits, which are very nourishing. We ought to be able to hold out quite a time, at least until Dr. Gambit is sensible enough to expel Natacha and Mrs. Van Tocht from the Institution."

Christabel handed us each a biscuit, which was neatly wrapped in soft paper. They were so small that each one would hardly have made a mouthful.

"You will find a scrap of paper in each biscuit with your fortune written on it," said Christabel. "I suggest each one of us reads out her own fortune."

Each person bit her biscuit in two and we read out our scraps of paper in turns. We were sitting in a circle around the pond. The order was moonwise. Veronica Adams, the Marquise, Anna Wertz, Georgina, Christabel Burns. I was last.

"Although you have given up hope, you will meet True Love again," read Veronica Adams.

"The battle is almost won, do not dissipate yourself unnecessarily. Victory is near." This was for the Marquise.

"Toil and Trouble will not always be your lot. A great change is imminent, be of good heart." Anna Wertz was about to make some commentary but Christabel held up her hand for silence, and she was accepted by mutual agreement as the head of the meeting. The candles guttered in a slight breeze.

"Your courage and goodwill are soon to reap a reward. Do not fear those who bear you ill will, they soon shall fall in shame," read Georgina, cackling with mirth. The next person was Christabel, who read: "Devotion and service to a holy cause is your destiny."

116

I unscrewed my own scrap of paper and read out: "Help! I am prisoner in the tower." There was a slight pause and Christabel, as if to avoid further discussion, pulled a very small tom-tom from under her shawl and began to pat it in rhythmic beats. We began by nodding our heads in time to the drumming, then our feet. Soon we were dancing round and around the pond, waving our arms and generally behaving in a very strange manner. At the time none of us seemed to find anything unusual about our weird dance. None of us felt tired. Even Veronica Adams, who was over ninety, pranced around as merrily as the rest. Never before had I experienced the joy of rhythmic dance, even in the days of foxtrot in the arms of some eligible young man. We seemed inspired by some marvellous power, which poured energy into our decrepit carcasses.

Christabel began to chant in time to the rhythm of her drums:

Belzi Ra Ha-Ha Hecate Come!
Descend on us to the sound of my drum
Inkalá Iktum my bird is a mole
Up goes the Equator and down the North Pole.
Eptàlum, Zam Pollum, the power to increase
Here come the North Lights and a flight of wild geese
Inkalá Belzi Zam Pollum the Drum
High Queen of Tartarus Hasten to Come

This chant was repeated time and time again till a cloud gathered over the round pond and we all shrieked in unison: Zam Pollum! Ave Ave Queen of all Bees!

Then it seemed that the cloud formed itself into an enormous bumble bee as big as a sheep. She wore a tall iron crown studded with rock crystals, the stars of the Underworld.

All this may have been a collective hallucination although nobody has yet explained to me what a collective hallucination actually means. The monstrous Queen Bee slowly revolved over the water, beating her crystalline wings so rapidly that they emitted a pale light. As she faced me I was thrilled to notice a sudden strange resemblance to the Abbess. At that moment she

closed one eye, as big as a tea cup, in a prodigious wink.

Then she slowly faded away, beginning with her barbed sting and ending with the tips of her curly antennae. A delicious scent of wild honey was left in the air.

For some miraculous reason nobody heard our revels. We all regained our respective bungalows unmolested, to fall into a deep dreamless sleep. Before we retired Christabel told us that we would meet again within three days, at midnight.

By mutual and silent consent we never discussed the apparition of Zam Pollum, the High Queen of Bees. Yet we were full of courage and determination to carry out our purpose.

Of course it was not easy to sit through all meals without tasting so much as a crumb of bread. Under the increasingly foreboding spectacle of Dr. Gambit we were obliged to renew our efforts continually. Hunger was also difficult to resist, as two biscuits a day did not really make a solid diet. Dr. Gambit gave us a lecture every day, to no avail. We were unmovable.

Mrs. Gambit did not tire of making caustic remarks through her agonized smile. None of us talked to either Natacha or Mrs. Van Tocht and I noticed they began to look haggard as time passed. They took to prowling around together and emerging in unexpected places, hoping no doubt to overhear our conversations. We were extremely prudent, and even Anna Wertz started speaking short sentences in an undertone.

Another matter made the hunger strike increasingly difficult. The weather had suddenly turned so cold that haw frost glittered over the garden every morning. This was a strange occurrence for a country beneath the tropic of Cancer. Towards midday the frost melted in the sunshine, but the days continued to get colder and in our underfed condition we suffered greatly. None of us possessed fur coats, so we would go around shivering in blankets. In spite of the hardships the sparkling white frost brought a strange joy into my heart, and I thought about Lapland.

We had all given up our morning tasks in the kitchen in spite of the efforts made by Mrs. Gambit to mobilize help. Since we ate nothing we could not be induced to work either. We had plenty of

time to wander around either talking, dreaming or occasionally thinking. Often enough I wondered about the message I had received in the biscuit. The more I thought about it the more urgent seemed those cryptic words: "Help! I am prisoner in the tower."

I had always suspected that somebody lived in the tower, but I had not the vaguest idea who that might be.

One day I met Christabel as I was looking for twigs to make a fire. We had taken to lighting bonfires in the garden to keep warm during the lunch hour. I took the opportunity to return the History of the Abbess and ask some questions. How, for instance, did the portrait of Doña Rosalinda come to be in America?

"That happened during the Spanish Civil War," replied Christabel, "a Spanish refugee called Don Alvarez Cruz de la Selva brought it into the country when he escaped the Fascists. He must have been a descendant of Doña Rosalinda and lived here for some years until he died and the house was taken over by the Gambits."

"Did they buy the house or did they rent it?" I asked Christabel.

"The Gambits rent the house from Alberto de la Selva, son of the original owner, who now runs a grocery store in the city."

"Do they also rent the tower?" I asked suddenly, and I noticed Christabel made a short pause before she replied: "The tower is never actually used by the Gambits. In fact half of it is inaccessible, because the staircase leading up to the tower room was walled up, with only a small barred window in the wall to allow ventilation."

"Christabel," I said, "Who lives in the tower?"

"I am not allowed to tell you," said Christabel. "That is something you have to find out for yourself. There are three riddles you have to answer before you are allowed to enter the tower. The first is:

'I wear a white cap on my head and my tail
All seasons my caps I wear without fail
Around my fat belly my girdle is hot
I move round and round tho' legs I have not.'

"The second riddle concerns the first and rhymes as follows:

'I never move as you whirl round and round
I sit and I watch you with never a sound
If you tilt far enough caps become belt
New caps are made the old caps will melt
Though legless your whirling will then appear lame
I seem to move but I don't, what's my name?'

"If you find the answer to the first riddle you ought to find the solution to the second. The third however is not so easy, although it still concerns the first and the second. It goes like this:

'One of you turns while the other will sit
And though the caps change they always will fit
Once in the life of a mountain or rock
I fly like a bird though bird I am not
When you get new caps my prison will break
The watchers who slept will now be awake
And over their land I will fly once again
Who is my mother? What is my name?'

"If you find the answer to these riddles you will understand who lives in the tower."

The weather had become so bitterly cold that we hastened to collect more twigs for the fire. The rest of our group, including Georgina, Veronica Adams, the Marquise, and Anna Wertz, had made a fine large fire on the lawn, and they were boiling water drawn directly from the warm spring which tasted slightly of sulphur. The Marquise had acquired some tea, which was a great luxury for us.

"Quite like old times," said the Marquise happily. "I bribed the gardener to buy us some tea, and since he could get us tea, I took the opportunity of getting two kilos of sugar."

"Sugar," we said in chorus. "O bravo!" Two kilos of sugar would probably save our life, as some of us were suffering so much from undernourishment that we feared pneumonia. Sugar would give us energy and help to keep us warm. The sweetened tea was

the most delicious elixir I had ever tasted.

In the afternoon there was a light snow fall and most of us were huddled under whatever covers we could find. Mrs. Gambit went to each bungalow telling us that Dr. Gambit wished to see us all assembled in the lounge, he had something particular to say. She was so unusually polite that some of us felt positively alarmed.

"Please sit down," said Dr. Gambit when we were all present, including Natacha and Mrs. Van Tocht. "What I have to say will not take long, but you might as well be comfortable, as I fear some of you may have lost strength during the last few days.

"Apparently there is some reason that prevents you from eating food in the dining room in the usual manner. I have done what I can to persuade you to eat it, to no avail. Owing to the unusually cold weather, lack of proper food may make you take risks which you do not fully realize.

"During this incomprehensible behaviour you have ostracized two of the community, Natacha Gonzalez and Mrs. Van Tocht, causing them great unhappiness. These two admirable and highly spiritual women have been so deeply pained by the aggressive attitude of the rest of the community that they have communicated with their respective families, who are arriving to take them away from the Institute tonight."

There was applause, but Dr. Gambit went on speaking without taking notice. "The lamentable result of your attitude towards two of the only people here who have benefited by the Work will be an irreparable loss to the Institute. I can only hope your own future remorse will finally be acute enough to make you realize the great injustice you have done to your two companions. That will be all at the present. I hope to see everybody seated in their usual places and eating normally at supper time."

Georgina very courageously got up and delivered the following speech as our spokeswoman: "Dr. Gambit, my companions and I have absolutely no remorse that the two females who we consider to be a public danger are being removed from our midst. We will assemble at meal times when we are perfectly sure that the food we are eating has not been tampered with. This will be twenty-

"As a matter of fact," said Carmella with dignity, "I have merely bought a limousine. Come and look at it." Drawn up in front of the main entrance was a huge long modern automobile painted a shade of lilac I knew to be Carmella's favourite colour. At the wheel sat a Chinese chauffeur in a black uniform powdered with pink roses. He saluted us respectfully.

I was so overcome with surprise that I could only wonder if the hunger strike had given me hallucinations.

"Majong," said Carmella to the chauffeur, "bring in the crate of sardines and the five dozen bottles of sweet port." The chauffeur leapt out of the car and started hauling out a crate from the luggage compartment, which started playing catatonic Sardanas, Carmella's favourite music, when opened.

With Carmella and I leading the way, Majong, the chauffeur, carried the luxurious crate, heavy with a hundred tins of real Portuguese sardines to my bungalow.

The snow that had started to fall during the afternoon had become heavier, and the garden was already white.

"Extraordinary weather for this time of year," said Carmella. "One would imagine oneself in Sweden. They say if the earth tilted the snow caps at the poles would melt and the equator would form new caps of snow, being in the place where the poles were before."

A great light flashed in my mind. The riddle, of course.

'I wear a white cap on my head and my tail
Around my fat belly my girdle is hot
I move round and round though legs I have not.'

The answer, of course, was the Earth. Why had I not thought of that at once? Then I felt suddenly afraid. Suppose my mother's idea that Monte Carlo was on the equator and that snow in Biarritz meant the poles were changing was really a prophecy? The effects of such a change would be disastrous to many inhabitants of the planet. My mind reeled.

"When I return tomorrow," said Carmella, "I will bring everybody sheepskin coats, just like mine, and top boots. It is a wonder that you don't all die of the cold."

"You mustn't spend all your fortune at once," I said. "It would be awful if you found you had nothing left after a week."

"Never mind," replied Carmella. "I have millions. I couldn't spend it all even if I wanted to. Just imagine, I have bought the biggest and most elegant tea room in the whole town, just as a present for my niece."

"But why don't you buy yourself a luxurious palace in town instead of coming here, where there is no luxury at all?"

"I like company," replied Carmella. "Besides I shall bring luxury with me. Like that mountain that went walking after somebody whose name I can't recall."

"It was Dunsanane Forest and Shakespeare said it went walking," I said, wondering if I might be mistaken.

"Forest or mountain, no matter," said Carmella, as we watched Majong arrange the bottles of port neatly along the walls of the Lookout. He put the precious crate of sardines on the table.

"It is so cold in here," said Carmella, "that I shall leave you my coat."

"Please do not, I would be very embarrassed," I said, hoping she would anyhow.

"I have a fine bearskin rug in the car," said Carmella, "Majong!"

"Yes Madam."

"Go and get the bearskin rug out of the car. I am leaving my cloak with Mrs. Leatherby. She will certainly catch pneumonia if she sleeps in here tonight without adequate covering."

"Yes Madam." He left as I protested feebly. The cold was most intense, and seemed to increase hour by hour.

"I really believe the poles are changing places," said Carmella. "There will almost certainly be famine, so I shall go shopping tomorrow morning and bring supplies. We will no doubt soon be fighting packs of hungry wolves." She seemed pleased at the thought and elaborated further, "Naturally elephants living in Africa and India would have to grow long fur and become mammoths again, to survive the cold. Flora and fauna of a tropical kind that were unable to adapt would perish. I feel most upset

125

about the animals. Happily most of them have fur that grows quickly, and carnivorous animals would have plenty of human beings to eat, all those people who had not foreseen what was coming and died of exposure. It is all the fault of that dreadful atom bomb they were so proud of."

"You mean we are entering another ice age?" I asked, feeling far from happy.

"Why not? it happened before," said Carmella logically. "I must say that I do feel it is poetic justice if all those horrible governments are frozen stark in their respective governmental palaces or parliaments. Actually they always sit in front of microphones, so there is a good chance that they might all get frozen to death. That would be a nice change, after pushing the poor nations to allslaughter, ever since nineteen fourteen.

"It is impossible to understand how millions and millions of people all obey a sickly collection of gentlemen that call themselves 'Government!' The word, I expect, frightens people. It is a form of planetary hypnosis, and very unhealthy."

"It has been going on for years," I said. "And it only occurred to relatively few to disobey and make what they call revolutions. If they won their revolutions, which they occasionally did, they made more governments, sometimes more cruel and stupid than the last."

"Men are very difficult to understand," said Carmella. "Let's hope they all freeze to death. I am sure it would be very pleasant and healthy for human beings to have no authority whatever. They would have to think for themselves, instead of always being told what to do and think by advertisements, cinemas, policemen and parliaments."

By this time Majong had returned with the rug. Carmella gave me her coat and she left wrapped in the rug, leaning on the arm of her Chinese chauffeur.

"I will be here at noon tomorrow," said Carmella over her shoulder. "Get them to sterilize that double bungalow. Its vibrations must be very diseased after the murder."

Carmella disappeared into the night and, comfortably wrapped in the warm cloak, I sallied forth to invite the ladies to an orgy of

sardines and port wine.

The doors of the bungalow and Natacha's igloo hung open and snow blew into the empty rooms. Natacha and Mrs. Van Tocht had gone. Where they had gone to we never discovered, and none of us made much effort to find out.

At dawn I arose and looked out. It was still snowing, and the pale garden looked delightful. I was surprised to see several ladies walking towards the main building at such an early hour. Perhaps they had decided to take breakfast in the dining room, as Natacha and Mrs. Van Tocht had gone. It was difficult to believe that they were unusually hungry, as we had dined royally on several tins of sardines each, washed down with fine sweet port. A banquet, in fact. However, after so many days fasting perhaps they still had a lot of appetite. I dressed slowly and thought about the two riddles I had not yet solved.

'I never move as you whirl round and round
I sit and watch you with never a sound,'

Now who could this possibly be? If the first verse referred to the earth, did the second, perhaps, refer to the sun? It did seem like a possibility, as the sun does appear to move, although the third line insists again that the sun "caps" change:

"If you tilt far enough caps become belt,
New caps are made the old caps will melt.'

The Belt meant the equator obviously, and the "New Caps" would be new poles formed on the old equator. If this made sense and was not a gratuitous obscurity to make things more difficult, then the Sitting Watcher who appears to move but does not could not mean the sun. The poles don't have to change place with the equator to make the sun appear to move, it does that anyhow.

'Though legless your whirling will then appear lame
I seem to move but I don't, what's my name?'

What indeed? And why does the whirling Earth appear lame? I could not find the solution, and really I felt too old to cudgel

my ancient creaking brain with riddles. Feeling slightly cross, I wrapped myself in the great sheepskin cloak and walked out into the snow. The sun had not yet risen, dawn seemed to be unusually long, but the sky was overcast and this would have obscured the sun in any case.

The snow was almost up to my knees, but it was powdery and dry due to the intense cold. I felt rather guilty wearing such a nice warm cloak when the others were wrapped in all sorts of old blankets. If Carmella did not bring the other cloaks, I thought, we could make ourselves waistcoats out of this big cloak. That would keep one's bronchial tubes warm. Chest disorders at our age were not to be taken lightly.

The only spot in the garden which showed green was a perfect circle around the sunken rocks where the warm spring leapt out from underground. The round green circle surrounding the dark warm depths looked curiously unnatural in the expanse of snow. The Gambits, I thought, should have had an indoor bath built, where we could bathe our rheumatic joints. The sulphuric water was surely good for rheumatism? Perhaps they did not like to spend so much money on a property that was not their own. The owner, however, could have made a nice spa, with a naturally warm spring right on his property. Perhaps he earned enough money already with his grocery store.

The Marquise caught up with me and we shared the shelter of the cloak. Her face was cobalt blue with cold.

"It is inexplicable," she shouted into my left ear.

"Yes indeed, I never saw such fickle weather at this time of year," I replied, adjusting my hearing trumpet, which I now always carried hung on a cord, Robin Hood style.

"Not fickle," said the Marquise, "I said inexplicable!"

"Yes, it is really inexplicable, although I expect the geologists will make some very satisfactory and incomprehensible reports," I replied. "So much snow below the tropic of Cancer must be very unusual."

"Not only the snow," replied the Marquise, "but also the fact

that it is now eleven o'clock in the morning and the sun has not risen!"

What was left of my sparse grey hair rose on my scalp. The sun had not risen. Something really cataclysmic must be afoot. I was terrified, but also excited.

A fire had been lit in the lounge, and all the ladies had clustered around the warmth with mugs of coffee. They were discussing the phenomenon with animation.

"I do hope sea lions will migrate here," Anna Wertz was saying, "they are so wonderfully clever. We could teach them tricks in the garden and they would eat some of the sardines."

"If the sun is really disappearing," said Georgina, "the only life left on this planet will be arctic fungus, and even that will disappear eventually." The general and immediate preoccupation concerned clothing. I proposed we should cut the cloak into sections, in case Carmella forgot to bring others as she had promised. We all agreed that this would at least protect our bronchial tracts.

"It would take some time before we were entirely overrun with giant polar bears," continued Anna Wertz, whose mind seemed to have coagulated on arctic animals. "Large polar bears might be formidable enemies, although personally I believe that all animals are friendly if treated unaggressively. One would initiate a very kind but cautious attitude towards them, leaving a bowl of milk out in the evenings or a slice of salted cod, of which they are very fond. Bit by bit they could be induced to allow themselves to be petted, and even sleep inside the bungalows, this would increase the warmth immensely. One or two polar bears the size of ordinary cart horses could generate a good deal or warmth."

"Talking of warmth," said Georgina, "I suggest we move our camp beds in here for the night and keep the fire going, otherwise none of us will live to tell the tale. We might be the last surviving human beings on earth."

The brass clock over the fireplace suggested that it was already midday, but the pale sun got no lighter and the snow fell without

abating. Outside the trees were already laden, and one or two banana palms had collapsed under the weight of snow.

Anna Wertz went to the kitchen and got some dry bread which she threw outside on the veranda for the birds.

"They feel so cold, poor things, and nothing to eat all of a sudden." Actually some pigeons, sparrows and a few ravens were walking about on the snow outside looking for food. In the trees birds would begin to twitter and then stop, undecided whether it was morning or evening. We could hardly tell ourselves, if it hadn't been for the brass clock.

Georgina had locked all the doors, in case we were visited by Dr. Gambit, who might object to the lighted fire.

"If he comes now with his beastly sermons," said Georgina, "we had better tie him up and gag him. After all, they are only two against six."

I had begun to worry about Carmella, who had promised to arrive by midday. The roads would already be covered with snow and might be difficult to negotiate in a car.

Perhaps she had overslept, thinking, as I had, that at eleven o'clock it was dawn.

More and more birds agglomerated on the lawn, and the most audacious of them hopped onto the veranda and started picking at the crumbs. We were startled to see a toucan and some parrots arrive, as well as sea birds such as gulls, pelicans and small white cranes that lived on the coast in the tropics.

Soon we were all standing at the window watching the sight. In the pale twilight it was not always possible to distinguish the breed of bird, but those that came close enough were quite visible against the snow.

All of a sudden the front door bell clanged loudly and the birds nearest the house rose into the air with fright. I went to the front accompanied by Georgina. We were happy to see Carmella's lilac limousine drawn up at the front door.

"Get the door open," said Carmella poking her head out of one of the windows. "We must drive the car into the garden and use the headlights, there may be no electricity for some time."

I noticed she wore a handsome new lilac wig, to match the car. It suited her better, I thought, than the other one, which had been rather intensely red. With much puffing and wheezing Georgina and I managed to open the great double doors which had no doubt remained closed since Don Alvarez de la Selva had died. Majong drove the car into the court yard where it slithered and stopped. The snow was already too deep to get it into the garden.

"It will be alright here," I told Carmella, "because we have taken over the lounge and do not intend to allow the Gambits to enter. Unless of course they come pacifically."

"Excellent," said Carmella. "If we gather in one place it will be easier to economize fuel."

Majong had opened the luggage carrier, which sang "Sardanas" tunefully, and was already extracting all sorts of packing cases. The inside of the car was also stuffed to the roof with sheepskin cloaks, top boots, oil lamps, oil, umbrellas, caps, jerseys, flower pots with plants, and twelve agitated cats amongst which I recognized my own with rejoicing.

When Carmella opened the door all the cats leapt out of the car and ran hissing angrily in all directions. "They will soon settle down and come into the house," said Carmella. "I have taken the precaution to put some dried codfish inside my cloak so they can find me easily by my scent. They won't get lost."

As Majong carried the packing cases into the house Carmella ticked off each item on a long list she carried in her hand.

"Mushroom spore. Beans, lentils, dried peas and rice. Grass seed, biscuits, tinned fish, miscellaneous sweet wines, sugar, chocolates, marshmallows, tinned catfood, face cream, tea, coffee, medicine chest, flour, violet capsules, tinned soup, sack of wheat, work basket, pick-axe, tobacco, cocoa, nail polish, etc. etc." There were enough provisions to face a siege.

"As soon as the sky clears we will use the planisphere," said Carmella. "And then we will know exactly what is happening. During the last three months I made friends with a student of astronomy who explained exactly how it works."

"You may be right about the changing of the poles," I said,

thinking of the strange riddles that Christabel had given me to solve. "The sun has not really risen since yesterday morning."

"It is surprising how friendly people become if you have money," said Carmella reflectively. "The astonomer actually wanted to marry me, but as he was only twenty-two I thought it would be imprudent. I don't really want to marry again in any case."

We stacked all the provisions in the lounge. It was not quite warm inside but the supply of wood that Mrs. Gambit had gathered in the closet was not large, and it was doubtful if it would last through another day or night. There was no coal, because in the past wood fires in the evening were quite sufficient to keep warm.

Carmella gave everybody sheepskin cloaks, top boots, woollen socks and caps. We looked like a gang of north pole explorers that had been stranded for half a century in the arctic circle.

"Majong will take charge of the kitchen," said Carmella. "He is a wonderfully economical cook."

"What about Mrs. Gambit?" said Georgina. "She'll be guarding the kitchen with her life."

"We will see, perhaps she would be pleased to have all the work taken out of her hands."

So we installed ourselves in the lounge. Night started to fall towards four o'clock in the afternoon, and the snow stopped.

Little by little the clouds blew away, revealing a magnificent clear dark starlit sky. Carmella unpacked the planisphere and we all set out into the garden to examine the stars. The planisphere was a disk of cardboard with a map of the stars seen from our portion of the globe, over which revolved another disk of plastic which had the stars invisible from our portion. There was what seemed to be a complicated system of months and hours around the circumference of the cardboard which somehow corresponded to the stars. In the centre of the disk was a small hole.

Carmella manipulated the disk with efficiency, quickly finding the date and hour.

"The Pole Star has to be seen through the centre of the disk,"

she told us. "That is how one finds the positions of the other celestial bodies, which are all in motion. The Pole Star would only seem to move if the poles of the earth actually tilted far enough to make a complete change in their magnetic position."

A voice in my head which did not seem to belong to me chanted:

'But I never move as you whirl round and round
I sit and I watch you with never a sound
If you tilt far enough caps become belt
New caps are made, old caps will melt
Though legless your whirling will then appear lame
I seem to move, but I don't, What's my name?'

The Pole Star, of course. Without the planisphere I could never have thought of it. Although I remembered being told when we first bought the planisphere that the centre had to be fixed on the Pole Star.

Carmella was examining the disk by the light of a torch. The Pole Star had already been found, but none of the other constellations were in their right places.

Curious pale flashes occasionally lit the sky. There was not a breath of wind, yet the trees were swaying and loads of snow rushed off the branches to the ground. Then we saw the house move against the sky. The trees shook with a force that might have been a strong wind. Yet the cold air was still. Rifts appeared in the snow, the house groaned as if in pain, and we heard objects falling.

"An earthquake!" shouted Georgina, clutching Veronica Adams to avoid falling. "Look at the tower!"

That portion of the building suddenly glowed red as if it was on fire. The great stone tower swayed from side to side, then the air was rent with the sound of a mighty crackling and the walls split open like a broken egg. One tongue of flame shot out from the crack like a spear, and a winged creature that might have been a bird emerged. It paused momentarily on the brim of the shattered tower and we witnessed for a second an extraordinary creature. It shone with a bright light coming from its own body, the body of a human being entirely covered with glittering feathers and armless.

Six great wings sprouted from its body and quivered ready for flight. Then with a shrill long laugh it leapt into the air and flew North, till it was lost to our sight.

'Once in the life of a mountain or rock
I fly like a bird though bird I am not'

Sephira, but who was the Mother of such a Son?

I saw Christabel watching me with a curious smile, and without further deliberation I said: "The Earth is the answer to the first riddle. The second is the Pole Star, and the third is Sephira, whose Mother I do not know."

She gave a high cackling laugh, which nobody heard but me because they were all gazing after the six-winged Sephira.

"Follow me," she said, "and you will know the Mother of Sephira who has now escaped to sow panic amongst the nations:

'The Watchers who slept will now be awake
And over their land I will fly once again
Who is My Mother? What is My Name?'

We left the group staring at the sky and made for the tower. All had become still, and the sky was clouding over preparing for more snow. Tufts of smoke issued from the great crack as we approached, and I thought it must be on fire. We gained access by the door which had been split off its hinges by the force of the earthquake. A strong smell of sulphur and brimstone hung on the air.

"Up or Down?" asked Christabel as we found ourselves inside. A winding staircase led up to the top of the tower. Part of the steps had crumbled away and through the great crack in the wall the night sky was visible now, moving with gathering clouds. At our feet yawned an opening where steps faded into darkness below. A warm wind that blew up from underground fanned our faces.

Up or Down? Before I gave a reply I leant over and tried to stare into the darkness. I could see nothing.

Then I turned my eyes up and saw some bright stars shining between the torn masses of cloud. It looked immeasurably far away and very cold.

134

"Down," I replied at last, because of the warm wind that blew from within the earth. Falling into a crematorium was still better than freezing to death on top of the tower.

I would have turned back, but curiosity went deeper than fear.

"You must go down alone," said Christabel, and before I could reply she had gone off into the night.

If the weather had not been so cold I might have returned even then. I was filled with terror. At that moment a chill wind blew under my cloak, and that made me start descending the stone stairs, very slowly.

The steps were rather wide. Nevertheless I was afraid of falling as it was so dark. I could not even see my own hand. However feeling about in the obscurity I found the wall, and I leant on it as I descended.

For a time the steps led straight downwards. Then we came to a sharp bend where the wall was rounded and smooth, as if many hands had rubbed it, just as my own. As I turned the bend with caution the darkness was expelled by a flickering glow like firelight. When I had gone down another twenty steps or so the ground evened out into a long gallery which looked over into a great round chamber hewn out of the rock. Carved pillars supported an arched roof which was faintly lit by the fire in the centre of the chamber. The fire seemed to burn with no fuel, it leapt directly out of a cavity in the rock floor.

At the farthest end of the gallery a final flight of steps led down into the large round chamber. As I reached the bottom of the steps I could smell sulphur and brimstone. The cavern was as warm as a kitchen.

Beside the flames sat a woman stirring a great iron cauldron. She seemed familiar to me, although I could not see her face. Something in the clothes and the bent head made me feel I had often seen her before.

As I drew near the fire the woman stopped stirring the pot and rose to greet me. When we faced each other I felt my heart give a convulsive leap and stop. The woman who stood before me was myself.

True, she was less bent than I and so her form seemed somewhat

taller. She may have been a hundred years older or younger, she had no age. Her features were identical to my own but her expression was much gayer and more intelligent. Her eyes were neither dim nor bloodshot, and she carried herself with ease.

"You took a long time to get here. I was afraid you might never come," she said. I could only mumble and nod, feeling my age upon me like a load of stones.

"What is this place?" I finally asked, shaking all over, feeling my knees would bend and crumble under my weight.

"This is Hell," she said with a smile. "But Hell is merely a form of terminology. Really this is the Womb of the World whence all things come." She stopped and looked at me inquiringly. I could see that she expected me to ask questions, but my mind was as numb as a hunk of frozen mutton. A question sprang to my mind, and although it seemed absurd I put it into words: "Who would I have met if I had gone to the top of the tower?"

She laughed, and I heard my own laugh, though it never could have rung so merrily.

"Who knows? Perhaps a lot of angels playing harps, or Santa Claus maybe."

Questions started to form, without my permission they jumped into my mind, each seemed sillier than the other. "Which of us is really me?" I asked aloud.

"That is something that you must decide first," she said. "When you have decided I will tell you what to do."

"Then would you like me to decide which of us is I?" she asked, and I thought that she looked so much more intelligent than I did that I replied, croaking: "Yes, Madam, will you please decide, my head is not as clear as usual this evening."

She looked me up and down from head to foot and then from foot to head, rather critically I thought, and said finally, as if to herself, "Old as Moses, ugly as Seth, tough as a boot and no more sense than a skittle. However meat is scarce so jump in."

"What?" I said, hoping that I had misunderstood. She nodded gravely and pointed into the soup with the long wooden spoon. "Jump into the broth, meat is scarce this season."

I watched in horrified silence as she peeled a carrot and two

onions which she tossed into the foaming pot. I never had any pretentions to a glorious death, but ending up as a meat broth had never entered my calculations. There was something paralysingly sinister in the offhand manner that she peeled the vegetables which were going to make my juice tastier.

Then, whetting the knife on the stone floor and smiling in a friendly manner, she approached me. "Not afraid surely?" she said. "Why, it won't take a moment, and after all it is your own decision. Nobody made you come down here did they?"

I tried to nod and move away at the same time, but my knees were trembling so much that instead of going towards the staircase I shuffled crabwise nearer and nearer the pot. When I was well within range she suddenly jabbed the pointed knife into my back side and with a scream of pain I leapt right into the boiling soup and stiffened in a moment of intense agony with my companions in distress, one carrot and two onions.

A mighty rumbling followed by crashes and there I was standing outside the pot stirring the soup in which I could see my own meat, feet up, boiling away as merrily as any joint of beef. I added a pinch of salt and some peppercorns then ladled out a measure into my granite dish. The soup was not as good as a bouillabaisse but it was a good ordinary stew, very adequate for the cold weather.

From a speculative point of view I wondered which of us I was. Knowing that I had a piece of polished obsidian somewhere in the cavern I looked around, intending to use it as a mirror. Yes, there it was, hanging in its usual corner near the bat's nest. I looked into the mirror. First I saw the face of the Abbess of Santa Barbara de Tartarus grinning at me sardonically. She faded and then I saw the huge eyes and feelers of the Queen Bee who winked and transformed herself into my own face, which looked slightly less ravaged, owing probably to the dark surface of the obsidian.

Holding the mirror at arm's length I seemed to see a three-faced female whose eyes winked alternatively. One of the faces was black, one red, one white, and they belonged to the Abbess, the Queen Bee and myself. This of course might have been an optical illusion.

I felt very well and refreshed after the hot broth, and somehow deeply relieved, just as I felt long ago after I had the last of my teeth out. I hitched my sheepskin cloak around me and went up the stone steps whistling Annie Laurie, which I thought I had forgotten years ago.

Ages seemed to have passed since somebody first hobbled down the steps, and now I was climbing to the upper world as spry as a mountain goat. The darkness was no longer a hideous death trap where any moment I might be precipitated to my death.

Strangely I could see through the dark like a cat. I was part of the night like any other shadow.

Outside the snow was falling abundantly once more and had already sprinkled white over the wrecked institute. The house had crumbled to the ground, leaving only two jagged walls standing above the decomposed pile. The building must have fallen after the second earthquake, which closely succeeded the first. I contemplated the ruins peacefully.

My companions had built a large fire on the snow-covered lawn and they were dancing around it to the sound of Christabel's tom-tom. It seemed a practical way to keep warm.

The Gambits must have been buried somewhere under the wreckage, but nothing moved, and the heaps of stone and mortar were being gently covered with snow.

I felt elated and mysterious and joined my companions in the dance around the fire. It was impossible now to tell the hour, as day had merged into night without the sun having risen at all.

"Did you enjoy the soup?" called Christabel as she thumped her drum, and the others laughed and repeated "Did you enjoy the soup?"

Then I understood that they all knew what had happened in the cavern chamber under the tower. We were quite warm and stopped dancing to regain our breath.

"How do you know I drank the broth?" I asked them, and they all laughed.

"You were the last to go down into the cavern," said Christabel. "All of us have been down into the underworld. Who did you meet?"

These were ritual questions and I understood that I must tell the truth.

"I met myself."

"Who else?" asked Christabel, as my companions clapped their hands rhythmically.

"The Abbess of Santa Barbara de Tartarus and the Queen Bee," I replied. Then with sudden curiosity I asked, "Who did you meet?"

And they all spoke together, "Ourselves, the Queen Bee and the Abbess of Santa Barbara de Tartarus!"

Then I also joined in the shrill laughter, and we set to dancing again to the sound of the tom-tom.

Nobody knew how much time went past before the sun rose again, but rise it did, pale white light near the horizon shining on a world transformed by the snow and ice.

As a result of the earthquake white ruins dominated the landscape. Not a whole house stood within sight, and many trees had been uprooted. Majong, Carmella's chauffeur, had survived the earthquake. He had taken refuge in the violet limousine, which had merely suffered a crushed engine. Nervous cats emerged from different corners, but all twelve were whole and unharmed. We dedicated the hours of sunlight to hunt amongst the ruins of the house for whatever food stuff we could find.

We transported it all down to the cavern chamber, which was warm with the fire that burned from the rocks. Christabel explained that this was natural gas and burned eternally. The hot spring which bubbled in the garden above had its source in the rocks under the tower.

There was no sign of any soup, but a disused iron cauldron stood near the fire. A sextagonal polished sheet of obsidian hung on the wall, and we all knew that it served as a mirror.

Days and nights were distributed unevenly. The sun never reached its zenith but sank at about midday. The earth seemed to be limping around its orbit seeking balance in the new order.

Soon enough we were nicely settled in the cavern chamber,

accompanied by all the cats and Majong, who had taken to talking entirely in Chinese. There was a certain amount of food, although many of the packing cases had been impossible to extract from under the wreckage of the building. Some sacks of lentils and wheat, mushroom spore and some badly squashed marshmallows were more or less the extent of our provision.

The violet limousine was beyond repair and would not have been much good in several metres of snow. We often went out from the cavern but we saw no human beings, though there were plenty of birds and animals in the region. Deer, pumas and even monkeys had come from the mountains and wandered about in the region looking for food. We did not consider hunting them. The New Ice Age should not be initiated with the slaughter of our fellow beings.

Majong transported earth down to the cavern, which he dug up near the warm spring, where the snow was soft and not frozen like everywhere else. We made a large garden of mushrooms, which flourished in all the warmth and dampness. This formed the main portion of our diet, and we carefully reserved a section for spore so that the crops would not decrease. Now and again we planted wheat, and were able to eat this when it germinated, but without sunshine it was impossible to propagate. One day we saw some goats grazing around the hot spring where a few twigs and grass still grew above the snow. This happy event provided the cats and ourselves with fresh milk. We pulled branches off the trees to provide provender for the goats, and they joined us later in the cavern, emerging now and again to look for food.

Each time the sun rose we went to the ruins looking for food, and these excursions were occasionally rewarded with crushed sardines or some handfuls of rice.

One dawn, we no longer used the word day, I was occupied digging under some frozen lumps that looked like a piece of furniture when I saw a sight so unusual that it frightened a flock of ravens off the portion of wall on the east side.

Walking along the faint track which once had been a road came the postman. He wore an ordinary postman's uniform and carried

a satchel for letters. The most remarkable object about him was the guitar slung over his shoulder. "Good day," he said, "I have some correspondence for this address," and he handed me a postcard of Marble Arch and some Life Guards.

This remarkable document read:

All in excellent health in spite of v. cold weather. Quite a sight skaters on the Channel. Madam and self watched ice hockey just off Dover Cliffs. Hoping all in g. health

Respectful regards Margrave.

"Of course correspondence is not so rapid any more, as I had to bring quite a lot over from England," said the postman. "I came on foot, or rather on skis."

"Are there many survivors?" I asked.

"Not many," said the postman. "Most of the big cities are overrun by abominable snowpeople. They don't do any harm, just picking around for food like everyone else."

"You must come down and take a glass of warm milk," I told the postman. "We will all be pleased to hear whatever news is going. We have seen no other human beings for a long time."

"I don't mind if I do," said the postman, following me and rubbing his hands.

Down in the cavern Anna Wertz was cooking some mushrooms in goat's milk, while Georgina and Veronica Adams were making a spinning wheel to weave goat wool. We were soon joined by Carmella, the Marquise, Christabel, and Majong who had been on an excursion to look for buried vegetables. They had found some carrots and frozen hay for the goats.

"My name is Taliessin," said the postman. "I have been carrying messages all my life, which has been a long one."

Anna Wertz gave him a cup of mushrooms and milk. He settled himself by the fire and began: "All nations and seas were shaken by earthquakes, which were so violent that not a house, castle, hovel or church was left standing. All this took place after days of snowfall and darkness. In some regions there was violent thunder and rain which froze as it fell from the sky. Spears of rain as tall as skyscrapers stood stiff over the snow. It was a rare sight. Herds of

wild and domestic animals galloped through the cities, uttering their different cries all at once and seeking shelter from the heaving earth. In some places fire leapt out of the earth and strange sights were seen in the sky. The surviving Humans were mostly overcome by panic and shock, although some were stalwart and tried to save the many million victims still alive under the fallen cities. Frightful scenes prevailed in the areas with many inhabitants."

"What of the Holy Grail?" asked Christabel.

"In Ireland," replied Taliessin, "the Earthquakes on the West coast were so violent that the air was full of rocks flying miles high. Volcanos sprouted out of the earth in six hundred different places, and snow and lava made a deadly soup which carried away men and beasts. Rains of moles, mice and small dead birds beat on the roofs and covered the streets and countryside a yard thick. During these cataclysmic convulsions the ancient fort of the Templars, the Rath of Conor, was blown into the air as if it were a kite. The Vault of the Arcanum was split asunder and the Grail was tossed into the air with the rest. The Holy Vessel landed intact on the straw roof of a half-destroyed peasant's dwelling. Here it was recovered by a peasant woman who put it in a wooden chest and took it to the parish priest, who was amongst the survivors of the cataclysm. The priest, a certain Father o'Grady, thought that the Sacred cup was a chalice of the kind used in the church, but of a somewhat eccentric design, and took it to Dublin where several bishops and a few Jesuits had taken refuge in a wine cellar. The explosion that had rent the Rath of Conor had momentarily dispersed the powers that always gathered around the Cup in enclosed areas. This is a magic law and true for nearly all charged objects. Consequently the Grail was desecrated in the hands of the clergy with impunity, enclosed in a packing case with straw, and debated upon as any ordinary antique. However amongst the Jesuits there was a certain learned man by the name of Rupert Traffix, who recognized the curious design of the Grail. His suspicion turned to conviction when he learnt from o'Grady that the Cup had been found in the precincts of the Rath of Conor. The

tower was known amongst certain scholars to have been the ancient dwelling of the Knight Templars.

"Darkness was dispersed in the midday sun that burned over the British Isles for twenty-nine hours, and the Jesuit escaped with the Grail to England. This was easy as the Bishops and the remaining Jesuits had imbibed so much wine without food that they were all lying in a drunken stupor. I was in the region of Rath of Conor during the explosion and followed the Grail to Dublin and then to England.

"Under the Bank of England the deep vaults served as a refuge for different powerful people such as men of state, wealthy business men, generals, and of course dignitaries of the church. During the last atomic war an underground town had been constructed to shelter lives considered precious by the government. The existence of this underground city was of course held secret, to prevent it being invaded by panic stricken masses of common people. This was the goal of the Jesuit, Rupert Traffix.

"Now in the precincts of Hampstead Heath there is a certain cavern used by a coven of witches who hold their ceremonies there in secret in order not to be molested by the law. From ancient times the witches had danced in the cavern through wars and persecutions; many a time when I was pursued I would hide with the witches, and was always received with courtesy and kindness. As you are no doubt aware, my mission through the ages has been to carry uncensored news to the people, without consideration of either rank or status. This has made me unpopular with the authorities all over this planet. My object is to help human beings to realize their state of slavery and exploitation by power-seeking beings.

"So when I arrived in London I took immediate refuge in the cavern on Hampstead Heath, amongst the witches. Here I learnt of the existence of a passage that communicated with the underground city beneath the Bank of England.

"There was much excitement in the coven when I informed them that the Holy Grail was already on the Island, and we made all kinds of plans to get it once more into our possession. As you

know, the Great Mother cannot return to this planet until the Cup is restroed to her filled with Pneuma, and under the guard of her consort the Horned God.

"Although we made many ingenious plans to recover the Grail we were unable to approach it. Finally our spies informed us that the Grail had left England in a seaplane, under the guard of several plainclothes policemen and Rupert Traffix the Jesuit. Further, that the destination of the Holy Cup was this very plateau; it was learned that earthquakes and volcanic eruptions had been milder on this part of the American Continent. Worshippers of the Revengeful Father God were of course determined to keep the Grail in their possession, and a small nucleus of initiates knew the magic of the Cup. These special initiates knew that their hypnotic power over humanity could not endure if The Great Mother was once more in possession. Rupert Traffix was among those who were fully informed of the history of the Cup.

"All this will explain why I am here and still in quest of the Holy Grail."

There was a short silence after all this momentous news, and Anna refilled our cups of mushrooms and goat's milk.

"We must make immediate plans to recover the Grail and restore it to the Goddess," said Christabel. "Her flight after the atomic war was the final nail in the coffin of this generation. If the planet is to survive with organic life she must be induced to return, so that goodwill and love can once more prevail in the world."

"In the city a few miles away," said Taliessin, "lies the Cup. Surviving worshippers of the Angry Father God are already being informed of its presence in this country and will eventually arrive here to try and save the last remnants of their demonological, sacrilegious religion."

"May the Queen Bee fill the Cup with Pneuma," said Christabel fervently.

"In Europe the Lion has finally dominated the countries and the Unicorn has flown in despair to Sirius," said Taliessin mysteriously. His words made the blood in our veins run cold.

"The Unicorns gone!" exclaimed Christabel in horror, for she

146

was the only one at that time to understand the full import of this terrible news; Taliessin bowed his head and replied, "Abomination and desolation on human kind."

"How can we recapture the Holy Cup?" asked Georgina, who was striding up and down nervously. "It must be well guarded?"

"We will make brews and ablutions to evoke the advice of Holy Hekate," said Christabel. "We must find stramonium, musk and vervaine and concoct a powerful soup, after making the necessary ablutions. Somewhere in the city there must be an accessible chemist's shop. Taliessin and Majong must set out after dark to bring the ingredients."

We all agreed to this plan; an invocation to the Goddess was the only chance of obtaining a clear indication of how we would gain possession of the Grail.

Taliessin and Majong armed themselves with tools from the destroyed limousine and set out for the city. A pale crescent moon flew amongst the clouds that were gathering for another snow storm.

While Christabel was practising some preliminary ablutions for the evocation a sudden disturbance became evident amongst the goats. They ran to the darkest extremity of the cavern chamber and started bleating piteously. Far away we heard the howling as if from a multitude of dogs.

"The poor things must be starving," said Anna Wertz after listening for a while. "We ought to take them some food." She then set about preparing a soup with boiled rice, some milk, and a few sardines to give a savoury taste.

When the soup was done Anna and the Marquise carried the cauldron to the upperworld. The howling of the dogs was now getting nearer and there was something in their tone that struck me as being not quite usual. When Anna and the Marquise eventually returned, the pot was empty.

"Poor things," said Anna. "I never saw such nervous hungry dogs. And just imagine, they were all Alsatians, but could not be induced to let me pet them. They fell on the food as if they had been starving for months. It really is a scandal the way people

neglect their animals. There they are all thinking about saving their own necks and letting their poor faithful dogs run around in herds, starving."

At that point we were all staring at the foot of the staircase. Anna had been followed by one of the dogs, a huge male greyish coloured Alsatian with nervous shifting eyes. I stood up, and as I approached the great beast flinched nervously aside. A frightful wail went up from the huddled goats. This was no dog, but a huge grey timber wolf.

Evidently this wolf was the head of the pack. More courageous than the rest, he had ventured down to the warmth of the cavern. We threw him some morsels of dried fish, which he took ravenously, watching us all the while with suspicious slanting eyes.

"He really is too hair-raisingly sweet," said Georgina, who had placed herself on the far side of the eternal fire. "I expect he would tear one's throat out by the roots in no time."

Anna kept approaching the wolf, almost as if she hoped to be bitten, "Poor boy! did they starve him to death? Well it really is a crying shame the way people treat dogs. After all no human beings are ever as nice as animals. For real understanding one can only depend on dogs." Nobody would ever convince Anna that this was not a dog but a wild beast from the distant woods.

The pack was still howling outside but I could tell that they had changed their chorus, and through a slight tingling on my scalp, I detected a new sound quite near and strangely reminiscent of mince pies. Although I was still in need of my trumpet I had recently developed a premonition of sound which I could translate afterwards through the trumpet.

"Surely it can't be Christmas?" said Carmella. Then I knew that what had joined the wolf chorus was the tinkling of many small bells, now clearly audible in the cavern. The wolf stood with ears alert, waiting.

"Darling! how too amazingly appropriate for the weather," remarked Georgina. "Dear old Santa Claus will come gallivanting in any minute, positively dripping toys and good cheer all over the place."

As a matter of fact this is almost what did happen. After a few minutes we heard a series of piercing whistles and a voice as if from the most remote and ancient past calling down the stone stairs: "Pontefact! Pontefact! what are you doing! you naughty wolf! come at once to father."

Marlborough's voice always carried further than anybody else's. Even in my deafest days I could always hear him talk several rooms away. Suddenly there he was on the steps, in some way changed, but more himself than ever. He was clad in maroon velvet, lined with dark fur which happened to be sable. A tall square cap was pulled low over his immensely wizened face, and a very long narrow beard reached almost to the toes of his damp tennis shoes. On each shoulder perched a white falcon.

The wolf now behaved with all the abandoned affection of a spaniel. He rolled on his back, waved his legs in the air and whined with delight.

"Marlborough!" I exclaimed. "I thought you were still in Venice!"

"Darling," said Marlborough as if we had seen each other yesterday. "I had a frightful time tracking you down, but I finally found Carmella's niece still alive in a bakery. The city really looks quite beautiful. All those awful houses have fallen down and everything looks as if it has teeth, with the icicles. Too strange for words."

"How did you get here from Venice?" I asked. "And what about your sister?"

"Anubeth came with me of course," said Marlborough. "She is upstairs in the Ark. I thought I would prepare you a little before introducing her. It might come as a surprise, although I know you don't expect anyone very normal. Please be careful not to hurt her feelings. After all you don't look so very ordinary yourself."

I introduced Marlborough to my five companions, and he walked around the cavern making appreciative exclamations, such as: "Really most exquisite proportion. One could feel oneself in a ziggurat. Darling, if you hung a rather long narrow gobelins with unicorns just off that corner it would give an entrancing trompe-oeuil, but I suppose the goats would eat it?"

"We haven't got any gobelins at the moment," I said, "but there is a nice bunch of straw which might do until we get one." Marlborough had stopped to pet the goats, who were still shuddering in a corner. Panic reigned again as the wolf, Pontefact, ran closely beside his master.

"Now were they afraid! Poor goats, poor pretty ones, dear Pontefact wouldn't do them any harm," murmured Marlborough in a comforting tone of voice. The goats would have none of it. "Dear Pontefact wouldn't harm anyone. Wolves are really cleverer than dogs. Besides Pontefact's father was a lamb, wasn't he darling?"

"I just adore your trousseau. Too utterly Chanel," said Georgina to Marlborough. "There is nothing like sable. So cosily chic. I suppose it was screamingly expensive?"

"I really don't know," said Marlborough. "Because I got it as a gift from the Princess Celina Scarlatti after I wrote her a bedroom sonata in *plain chant*. She had the costume made for herself when she tried to organize a fancy dress ball in the Vatican in aid of destitute lesbians. The Pope was very stuffy about the whole proposition."

"Marlborough," I said, "do you think you ought to leave your sister outside so long? She must be freezing to death."

"Anubeth is very patient," said Marlborough. "Besides the Ark has central heating and we have lived in it for months. We came overland via Canada because of the wolves. Anubeth is very fond of wolves. You will understand later. She had become very lonely in Venice, and when the snow started like called to like." This was all very mysterious. I had begun to anticipate the meeting with Marlborough's sister with a mixture of curiosity and dread.

"Perhaps we had better invite her down anyhow," I said. "It doesn't seem very polite to leave her alone in the upperworld."

While we climbed the steps Marlborough told me how they had journeyed from Venice through Italy and France and England, and finally over the North Sea to Canada.

Outside the tower stood Marlborough's Ark. I must say it was a most impressive sight. It was mounted on runners like a sledge, but otherwise it looked like a Renaissance version of Noah's Ark,

gilded, carved and painted in gorgeous colours, like a painting by a mad Venetian master. The whole contraption was covered with bells that tinkled frenetically with every gust of wind.

"Atom-propelled impulsion," said Marlborough proudly. "The whole engine fits into a rock crystal case no bigger than a hen's egg. It is the most modern form of mobile vehicle. No fuel, no noise. In fact it is so noiseless that I had to put the bells on to keep me company. How do you like it?"

"It's very gaudy," I said in admiration. "I suppose you had it made in Venice?"

"My own design," said Marlborough. "Gypsylike simplicity and atomic comfort."

The wolves sat around the Ark in a semicircle as if on guard. They made me feel nervous, although Marlborough assured me that they were perfectly tame. I also felt preoccupied about the cats that had disappeared at the first appearance of Pontefact.

"Excuse me while I call my sister," said Marlborough, and cupping his hands to his mouth he uttered a series of blood curdling yelps. These were answered from the interior of the Ark by more yelps and the rattling of the entrance door, which was tastefully carved with cupid and psyche embraced in the midst of stags and swans.

"Don't be afraid," said Marlborough. "If you let her see you feel anything unusual she gets very nervous."

The form which then emerged from the Ark was more wildly unexpected than anything my already inflamed imagination could have conceived. Marlborough's sister Anubeth was a wolf-headed woman. Her tall body was finely proportioned and, apart from the head, entirely human. She was swathed in some glittering cloth, and small pointed shoes like gondolas covered her narrow feet. She stood in the open door of the ark, growling and showing pointed white teeth. Marlborough growled back, which left me out of the conversation.

"My sister understands ten different languages and writes Sanskrit," said Marlborough, "but owing to a certain peculiarity of the palate she finds difficulty in pronunciation, so we always

bark at each other. You however may talk English to her, which she understands perfectly."

"How do you do?" I said nervously. "You are very welcome to our abode." Marlborough's sister growled. Later on I learnt a few intelligent phonetic phrases of Wolvery but at that time I found the conversation embarrassing.

"Anubeth asks if you would like to see inside the Ark," said Marlborough. "She is very house-proud and I must say she has arranged everything with great taste."

"Enchanted," I replied with a stiff bow. I found one was apt to address Anubeth with a certain ceremony, she was very imposing.

The interior of the Ark was like the opium dream of a gypsy. There were embroidered hangings of wonderful design, perfume sprays shaped like exotic feathered birds, lamps like praying mantis with moveable eyes, velvet cushions in the form of gigantic fruits, and sofas mounted on prostrate werewomen beautifully sculptured in rare woods and ivory. All sorts of mummified creatures hung from the roof, molded in such skillful gestures that they seemed alive.

"Anubeth likes to embalm anything she finds dead," said Marlborough. "This is her hobby. She uses a very ancient Egyptian technique. All our family are artistic."

Anubeth growled and reached up to get a very strange animal from the ceiling for my inspection. It was a tortoise with a baby's wizened face and long thin legs which were frozen in a gallop. "Anubeth says that this is a kind of collage she made for fun when the keeper of the principal morgues in Venice gave her the present of a dead baby. The legs originally belonged to some storks that died of the cold. It really is very clever. I sometimes wonder if she ought to paint. I am sure she has talent."

Here Anubeth and Marlborough exchanged several growls and we all sat down around a small jade table which was balanced on top of a reared cobra in amethyst.

"I must say you have made everything very comfortable and original," I told Marlborough. "This must really be the ideal form of travel." Anubeth served us some jasmine tea and small glasses of

a French liqueur whose name was fine champagne although it tasted nothing at all like champagne.

"Yes," said Marlborough who was comfortably settled on some velvet nectarine shaped cushions. "Our family have always been addicted to travel. In the past you even compared me to a swallow with my comings and goings. I believe I also inherit characteristics of Great Uncle Imrés, a Hungarian nobleman whose Mother was a well-known Transylvanian Vampire. For various reasons I have never told you my entire family history, as I was sworn to secrecy during the Communist persecution of Hungary. Now, sadly enough, the only remaining members of our family are Anubeth and myself. As I suggested before, I had a somewhat tense relationship with my other sisters, Audrey, Anastasia and Annabelle. They all suffered from a common mania, namely that when I crossed half the world to visit them in their respective castles, that my journeys were made with the object of stealing an early model vacuum cleaner which they were in the habit of hiring to each other at exorbitant prices. They all perished during the cataclysm. Audrey was found congealed upside-down in a small iceberg that invaded her bedroom. She was still holding an empty bottle of champagne to her lips. Very tragic, but not altogether without poetic justice. Physically speaking Anubeth was the only one of us to inherit characteristics of Great Uncle Imrés. He was a werewolf."

"Of course I understand that Communists must have objected very strongly to a werewolf, especially as he came from such a noble family," I said. Anubeth looked pleased and passed a long pink tongue over her jaws.

"Our property in Hungary was confiscated," continued Marlborough. "Uncle Imrés was caught and exhibited in a cage in St. Petersberg until he died of shame, then they had him stuffed and put in the Natural History Museum. All this had a devastating effect on our family pride. I published a short and rather bitter elegy to the memory of Great Uncle Imrés. You understand that the wolf blood in our family was something of a secret, although personally I consider it a distinction."

"It would be a great pity if werewolves died out altogether," I said. "After all animal-headed Goddesses and Gods have inspired us all through history."

Marlborough sipped his jasmine tea delicately and stroked his incredibly long beard. "As a matter of fact it was rather to prevent

such a calamity that we initiated our journey," he said. "You see Anubeth is now nearly eighty and we decided she should marry before it was too late to propagate the species. This is why we had to journey through Canada to find the Wolf King, Pontefact, who was happy to make the match."

"I beg your pardon?" I said, feeling astonished. "You mean?"

"Yes indeed," said Marlborough. "Anubeth is now happily married to King Pontefact whom you have already met. They are expecting a litter very soon. The whole wolf pack are Pontefact's subjects, so of course they accompany us everywhere."

I remained silent a while in order to digest this startling news. Would one refer to the litter as Babies? Werelets? or Puppies? I decided not to mention anything until Marlborough gave me a lead. In some things he was extremely conventional.

"I must offer you my hearty congratulations," I said to Anubeth. "We will all be happy to have young ones amongst us."

Marlborough told me that his sister and he would continue to live in the Ark because the presence of the wolves might upset the goats, and no doubt also because the comfort they enjoyed in the Ark was superior to the bare cavern where we lived, although he was too polite to say so. I asked them to dispose of any service we could offer and left them in a mist of white ginger perfume which issued from the beak of an embalmed cuckoo.

The wolves watched me as I picked my way cautiously out of their circle, I did not want to offend anybody, and wolves have notoriously quick tempers.

Below in the cavern I heard the sound of Christabel's drum which announced the return of Majong and the postman Taliessin. They had successfully broken into a collapsed pharmacy, where the required ingredients were found after some difficulty. The china pot containing the stramonium was somewhat chipped but the contents were still intact. After performing certain ablutions over us all Christabel emptied the contents of the three jars into the boiling cauldron.

Moonwise the dance began, and we were quickly lashed into a frenzy by the rhythm of Christabel's drum and the powerful vapours from the stramonium, vervaine, and musk boiling in the pot. The goats pranced around us in an outer circle, bleating.

Taliessin and Majong had retired to the upper world, as men were not allowed to see this magic ceremony.

"Belzi Ra Ha-Ha Hecate Come!
Descend upon us, the sound of my drum.
Inkalá Iktum my bird is a mole
Up goes the equator and down the North Pole!
Eptalum Zam Pollum the Power to increase
Here come the North Lights and a flight of wild Bees."

The air was filled with a humming and a drumming of wings, and millions of bumble bees gathered over our heads and formed a great female figure over the boiling cauldron. The swarm shimmered and shook in the formation of the giantess.

"Speak Zam Pollum!" cried Christabel. "Zam Pollum speak! Open your heart of wild honey and tell us how to capture your most Holy Grail that Earth shall not die on her axis! Speak Zam Pollum!"

The figure buzzed and shimmered, then somewhere from the depths of the body made from so many millions of bees came a voice so unbearably sweet that we felt drowned in honey.

"Bees shall nest again in the Lion's carcass. So my cup will be filled with honey and I shall drink again with the horned god Sephira the Pole Star, my husband and my son. Follow the swarm."

The circle of goats now dispersed in alarm as Anubeth joined our circle, walking majestically and bearing a lighted taper of incense.

"I am Anubeth, High Queen of the Wolves. My people wish to offer themselves to recover your most Holy Cup, Great Goddess Hekate Zam Pollum!" she said in Wolvery. The Goddess hummed with a million voices and drops of honey fell like manna from the roof of the cavern. We were covered with a most delicious perfumed stickiness and were obliged to lick ourselves clean.

The Swarm now dispersed, breaking the body of the Goddess into millions of shining fragments flying up the steps. "Follow!" called Christabel, and still dancing, we were drawn in the wake of the bees.

Then, spurred by a long howl from Anubeth the whole pack of wolves trailed behind us, and Marlborough's Ark left with all the bells tinkling wildly in chorus with the bees.

This is how the Goddess reclaimed her Holy Cup with an army of bees, wolves, six old women, a postman, a Chinaman, a poet, an atom-driven ark, and a werewoman. The strangest army, perhaps, ever seen on this planet.

The Marquise, who was in charge of the military organization

of the invasion, ordered the wolves to surround the palace of the Archbishop where the Grail was captive. In the meantime we would all start screaming that we were being attacked by wolves. As soon as the door opened the swarm of bees would rush into the palace and take the Cup from wherever it lay hidden.

All worked according to plan. The Archbishop himself ran downstairs to open the door as soon as we all started shrieking. Propelled by a supernatural intelligence, the swarm of bees whirled into the house and returned in a few moments carrying the Holy Grail, which they bore off to some secret part of our cavern, leaving a trail of honey in their wake which glittered like gold on the snow.

In a matter of seconds the Archbishop aroused the household, and soon a stream of infuriated ecclesiastics and secret police chased out into the garden. They were beaten back by the wolves and we made good our escape, with the pack bringing up the rear.

This is the end of my tale. I have set it all down faithfully and without exaggeration either poetic or otherwise.

Soon after the capture of the Grail, Anubeth was delivered of a litter of six young werewolf cubs which improved in appearance after their fur grew. Custom being a wonderful thing in its way, the cubs were soon playing happily with the kittens, while King Pontefact smiled wolfishly at his merry brood.

Ice ages pass, and although the world is frozen over we suppose someday grass and flowers will grow again. In the meantime I keep a daily record on three wax tablets.

After I die Anubeth's werecubs will continue the document, till the planet is peopled with cats, werewolves, bees and goats. We all fervently hope that this will be an improvement on humanity, which deliberately renounced the Pneuma of the Goddess.

According to Carmella's planisphere we are now somewhere in the region where Lapland used to be and this makes me smile.

A shewolf in the pack gave birth the same day as Anubeth to six white woolly puppies. We are thinking of training them to draw a sledge.

If the old woman can't go to Lapland, then Lapland must come to the Old Woman.

CITY LIGHTS PUBLICATIONS

Angulo, Jaime de. *JAIME IN TAOS*
Antler. *FACTORY (Pocket Poets #38)*
Artaud, Antonin. *ANTHOLOGY*
Baudelaire, Charles. *INTIMATE JOURNALS*
Bowles, Paul. *A HUNDRED CAMELS IN THE COURTYARD*
Breá, Juan & Mary Low. *RED SPANISH NOTEBOOK*
Brecht, Stefan. *POEMS (Pocket Poets #36)*
Broughton, James. *SEEING THE LIGHT*
Buckley, Lord. *HIPARAMA OF THE CLASSICS*
Buhle, Paul. *FREE SPIRITS: Annals of the Insurgent Imagination*
Bukowski, Charles. *THE MOST BEAUTIFUL WOMAN IN TOWN*
Bukowski, Charles. *NOTES OF A DIRTY OLD MAN*
Bukowski, Charles. *SHAKESPEARE NEVER DID THIS*
Bukowski, Charles. *TALES OF ORDINARY MADNESS*
Burroughs, William S. *ROOSEVELT AFTER INAUGURATION*
Burroughs, William S. *THE BURROUGHS FILE*
Burroughs, W. S. & Allen Ginsberg. *THE YAGE LETTERS*
Carrington, Leonora. *THE HEARING TRUMPET*
Cassady, Neal. *THE FIRST THIRD*
Charters, Ann, ed. *SCENES ALONG THE ROAD*
CITY LIGHTS JOURNAL No. 4
Codrescu, Andrei. *IN AMERICA'S SHOES*
Corso, Gregory. *GASOLINE/VESTAL LADY ON BRATTLE*
 (Pocket Poets #8)
David Neel, Alexandra. *SECRET ORAL TEACHINGS IN TIBETAN*
 BUDDHIST SECTS
Di Prima, Diane. *REVOLUTIONARY LETTERS*
Doolittle, Hilda. *(H.D.) NOTES ON THOUGHT & VISION*
Duncan, Isadora. *ISADORA SPEAKS*
Eberhardt, Isabelle. *THE OBLIVION SEEKERS*
Fenollosa, Ernest. *THE CHINESE WRITTEN CHARACTER AS A*
 MEDIUM FOR POETRY
Ferlinghetti, Lawrence. *LEAVES OF LIFE*
Ferlinghetti, Lawrence. *PICTURES OF THE GONE WORLD*
 (Pocket Poets #1)
Ferlinghetti, Lawrence. *SEVEN DAYS IN NICARAGUA LIBRE*
Gascoyne, David. *A SHORT SURVEY OF SURREALISM*
Ginsberg, Allen. *THE FALL OF AMERICA (Pocket Poets #30)*
Ginsberg, Allen. *HOWL & OTHER POEMS (Pocket Poets #4(*
Ginsberg, Allen. *INDIAN JOURNALS*
Ginsberg, Allen. *IRON HORSE*
Ginsberg, Allen. *KADDISH & OTHER POEMS (Pocket Poets #14)*
Ginsberg, Allen. *MIND BREATHS (Pocket Poets #35)*

Ginsberg, Allen. *PLANET NEWS (Pocket Poets #23)*
Ginsberg, Allen. *PLUTONIAN ODE (Pocket Poets #40)*
Ginsberg, Allen. *REALITY SANDWICHES (Pocket Poets #18)*
Herron, Don. *THE LITERARY WORLD OF SAN FRANCISCO &
ITS ENVIRONS*
Hirschman, Jack. *LYRIPOL (Pocket Poets #34)*
Horowitz, Michael. *BIG LEAGUE POETS*
Kerouac, Jack. *BOOK OF DREAMS*
Kerouac, Jack. *SCATTERED POEMS (Pocket Poets #28)*
Kovic, Ron. *AROUND THE WORLD IN EIGHT DAYS*
La Duke, Betty. *COMPAÑERAS: Women, Art, & Social Change
in Latin America*
Lamantia, Philip. *BECOMING VISIBLE (Pocket Poets #39)*
Lamantia, Philip. *MEADOWLARK WEST*
Lamantia, Philip. *SELECTED POEMS (Pocket Poets #20)*
Lowry, Malcolm. *SELECTED POEMS (Pocket Poets #17)*
Lucebert. *NINE DUTCH POETS (Pocket Poets #42)*
Ludlow, Fitzhugh. *THE HASHEESH EATER*
McDonough, Kay. *ZELDA*
Moore, Daniel. *BURNT HEART*
Mrabet, Mohammed. *M'HASHISH*
Murguía, A. *VOLCAN: Poems from Central America*
Newton, Huey & Ericka Huggins. *INSIGHTS & POEMS*
O'Hara, Frank. *LUNCH POEMS (Pocket Poets #19)*
Olson, Charles. *CALL ME ISHMAEL*
Orlovsky, Peter. *CLEAN ASSHOLE POEMS & SMILING VEGETABLE
SONGS (Pocket Poets #37)*
Pickard, Tom. *GUTTERSNIPE*
Plymell, Charles. *THE LAST OF THE MOCCASINS*
Poe, Edgar Allan. *THE UNKNOWN POE*
Prévert, Jacques. *PAROLES (Pocket Poets #9)*
Rey-Rosa, Rodrigo. *THE BEGGAR'S KNIFE*
Rigaud, Milo. *SECRETS OF VOODOO*
Rips, Geoffrey. *UNAMERICAN ACTIVITIES*
Rosemont, Franklin. *SURREALISM & ITS POPULAR ACCOMPLICES*
Sanders, Ed. *INVESTIGATIVE POETRY*
Shepard, Sam. *FOOL FOR LOVE*
Shepard, Sam. *MOTEL CHRONICLES*
Snyder, Gary. *THE OLD WAYS*
Solomon, Carl. *MISHAPS PERHAPS*
Solomon, Carl. *MORE MISHAPS*
Voznesensky, Andrei. *DOGALYPSE (Pocket Poets #29)*
Waldman, Anne. *FAST SPEAKING WOMAN (Pocket Poets #33)*
Waley, Arthur. *THE NINE SONGS*
Yevtushenko, Yevgeni. *RED CATS (Pocket Poets #16)*